P9-DOB-848

OVER THE MOON

OVER THE MOON

ELISSA HADEN GUEST

WILLIAM MORROW AND COMPANY, INC. / NEW YORK

Grateful acknowledgement is made to the following authors and publishers for the use of copyrighted materials:

Belwin-Mills Publishing Corp. for the excerpt from "Stormy Weather," Copyright © 1933 by Mills Music, Inc. Copyright renewed. Exclusively controlled by Mills Music, Inc. for the world, excluding the United States. All rights reserved. Used with permission.

CBS Songs for the excerpt from "Singin' In The Rain," words by Arthur Freed, music by Nacio Herb Brown © 1929, renewed 1957 Metro-Goldwyn-Mayer Inc. Rights assigned to CBS Catalogue Partnership. All rights controlled and administered by CBS Robbins Catalog, Inc. All rights reserved. International Copyright secured. Used by permission.

Chappell/Intersong Music Group for the excerpt from "Pennies From Heaven," Copyright © 1936 by Select Music Publications, Inc. Copyright renewed, assigned to Chappell & Co., Inc. (Intersong Music, Publisher). International Copyright Secured. All rights reserved. Used by permission.

Warner Bros. Music for the excerpt "Someone To Watch Over Me," © 1926 (Renewed) WB Music Corp. All rights reserved. Used by permission.

Inquiries should be addressed to
William Morrow and Company, Inc.,
105 Madison Avenue,
New York, NY 10016.
Printed in the United States of America.
1 2 3 4 5 6 7 8 9 10

Library of Congress Cataloging-in-Publication Data
Guest, Elissa Haden.
Over the moon.
Summary: Over protests from her family, sixteen-year-old Kate makes a difficult journey to see her beloved older sister, who ran away without explanation four years before.
[1. Sisters—Fiction] I. Title.
PZ7.G93750v 1986 [Fic] 85-28505
ISBN 0-688-04148-5

For my mother and father,
and my brothers, Nicky and Chris,
and for Cissy.

Acknowledgments

Many thanks are in order here. To David Reuther for his supreme patience and expertise. To Phyllis Wender for her continual support and enthusiasm. And to Jenny B. Gould, Jill Demby, and Meg Blackstone for their great help and advice in matters pertaining to the stuff of life.

Most of all I'd like to thank my husband, Nick, for everything.

Prologue

My sister Mattie was sixteen when she ran away with Dean Hartwell. They took off in the middle of the night on his Triumph motorcycle, a great, powerful machine of chrome and black. It was July when they left, just two weeks before my twelfth birthday. And I often thought back then that I could have forgiven her leaving, if only she'd waited until after my birthday.

I was not close to Mattie, but when she left us, I missed her in a deep, strange way. It was not a daily missing, and it was not often conscious, but I felt the mystery of her settle in my bones, her inner voice just under my own breath, her heartbeat wedged somehow between my own confused rhythm.

She was very beautiful, my sister, with light eyes and auburn hair. But there was a restlessness about

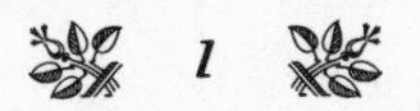

her, a sense of darkness that kept one from getting too close.

When she ran away, my aunt Georgia almost lost her mind.

"She was always so wild," she'd cried. "Always had a wild streak in her." And I'd pictured Mattie's soul as a canvas, a streak of midnight blue across her heart.

"Don't worry, the police will find them," my older brother Jay had said, doing his best to console her.

"She doesn't want to be found," I'd said. "That's why she ran away." I'd imagined her stealing away while we were sleeping. Moving through the dark at such a speed, her arms tight around Dean's waist, clinging, the air around them full of summer.

"Maybe she's only going for a little while," Jay had said. "You never know with Mattie, she could come back tomorrow." But I knew she wouldn't. I knew from the way she'd been acting those past few weeks. She couldn't wait to leave.

Mattie's room was above my own. It was the attic, really, and it had a wonderful sloped ceiling with wooden beams. She had painted the floor herself with white deck paint (against everyone's advice), and we all had to take off our shoes before entering.

"You have the best room," I once told her.

"Your room is nice," she said.

"Yes, but yours is so private, tucked away up here like a secret."

"I like it because it feels close to the sky," she said.

3

I loved Mattie's room. It was full of little odds and ends she'd collected over the years: a baby's shoe, an antique rocking horse, a basket filled with dried purple flowers. Next to a window was a watercolor by my mother called *Central Park in the Spring.* Underneath that was a photograph of my father holding Mattie when she was three months old. On one side of the room was an old Singer sewing machine. And on her desk, which was cluttered with notebooks and drawings, she'd kept a small bowl filled with the blue-and-green beach glass she'd picked the summer before our parents died.

Mattie used to spend whole days at a time in her room, listening to music, drawing, or writing in her diary. But that was before Dean came into the picture and turned everything upside down. After she met him she was hardly ever home, and she almost never spent any time alone in her room. Late at night I would lie on my bed and listen to her pacing up and down, the floor creaking under her bare feet. I could smell the smoke from her exotic cigarettes, Balkan Sobranies, filtering down through the vent in the wall. I could almost hear her thinking. In the daytime she was as drawn and tense as a cat about to spring. And every morning it seemed there was a fight with Georgia.

"What's wrong with him?" Mattie would shout.

"He's bad news," Georgia would say.

4

“How can you say that, you don’t even know him. You won’t even *try* to know him.”

“For starters he’s too old for you.”

“That’s not—”

“What is a twenty-eight-year-old man doing with a sixteen-year-old girl? Will you *please* tell me that?”

“Mom was only sixteen when she met Dad.”

“It’s not the same.”

“Why not? Why isn’t it the same?” And on and on and on.

Dean with his black leather jacket and dark, chiseled good looks. His voice had the smooth, seductive tone of a deejay caressing his listeners late at night. It was as if he wanted something from you and knew he could get it. It was so obvious to everyone but Mattie—he was not someone to trust.

It might not have been so odd if Mattie had gone away to school, if I’d known she was coming back for Christmas or spring vacation. But to have her leave in desperation, in anger, cast a pall over the rest of us. And months later, even when she wrote that she was safe, that she’d married Dean and was living down South, even then the three of us were left, bereft and shaken, each of us secretly afraid we were responsible for her going. We loved her too much.

CHAPTER ONE

Today I'm sixteen. I'm the same age my mother was when she met my father. I stare at myself in the mirror. I don't look any older, but it's an internal feeling, like switching gears on a bicycle. There's that quiet click, and then the motion beneath you is altered.

Last night I awoke to thunder and lightning. I sat up in the dark. A summer storm. The door flew open and my brother Jay came in.

"Do you believe this?" he said with a smile on his face. "It's fantastic."

"I just woke up," I said in a froggy voice. Jay had a blanket wrapped around his shoulders, and he came and sat next to me.

"Don't know why there's no sun up in the sky," he sang, "stormy weather!"

"Oh, Jay." White-gold lightning lit the sky. There

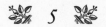

was a clap of thunder directly above us; my hands flew to cover my ears.

"Mother Nature doesn't kid around when it comes to your birthday," he said.

The next morning I didn't go to work as I do most Saturdays, in Georgia's store. She left me a note that said, "Happy Birthday, Cookie. I'll see you tonight. Love, Aunt G."

All morning Jay and I slapped down cards on the blue-and-white checked tablecloth. A vase of yellow roses stood in the center of the table like a small sun. The kitchen windows were foggy. We listened to the radio and drank lots of tea, and the rain went on and on. At noon I braved the storm and went down the hill to the mailbox. It was empty.

"No mail," I said to Jay.

"It'll probably come later today," he said. "How about another round of gin rummy?"

"All right."

In the afternoon we moved onto Monopoly, and around six or so, the rain began to let up and my friend Celia came over.

"Well, well, fabulous weather we're having, isn't it," she cried from the hallway. "All of Massachusetts must be drowning." We heard the front door slam behind her as she came in carrying a plastic shopping bag.

"Happy, happy birthday," she said, throwing her arms around me, getting me all wet. She was wearing her yellow slicker with a matching rain hat.

"Thank you," I said. "Actually, I sort of like this weather."

"Of course you do. It appeals to your dark, somber side."

"Want some tea?" Jay asked.

"Sure. Monopoly!" she said, aghast. "You can't play Monopoly with two people."

"You can if you're desperate," Jay said.

"By the way"—Celia turned to me—"are you planning to get dressed today?" I hugged my flannel robe around me. I loved sleeping wear: pajamas, bathrobes, comfortable clothes.

"I don't know. I may turn out to be one of those eccentric people who go everywhere in their pajamas."

"Why not?" she said.

"Did you walk all the way?" Jay asked.

"Yes, my mother's still getting the car fixed." Celia lived a mile and a half down the road from us.

"Listen, I have to talk to you, Jay," she said. "In *private*." She took his arm and half pulled him out of the kitchen. I heard them whispering.

"What's going on?" I shouted.

"It's a secret," she said.

"I don't like secrets."

"Who does?" she yelled back. After a minute they came back in. Celia had a big smile on her face. "I'd like you to go out now," she said to me.

"You would?"

8

"Yes, it's almost stopped raining, and I think you should take a nice long birthday walk."

"Alone?"

"I'm afraid so. We have work to do here."

"All right," I said, "but I hope you didn't invite anyone over for supper."

"Don't you trust me?"

"No!"

I went upstairs. My bed was still unmade, and there was clothing on the floor. My room was square and light with two big windows overlooking Georgia's rose garden. Pictures of foreign countries from *National Geographic* were pasted all over the walls, and an enormous map of the world hung over my bed.

I dressed quickly, putting on an old T-shirt and faded jeans, the softest clothes next to pajamas. Downstairs in the hall I slipped on my rubber boots and reached for an old raincoat that had belonged to Georgia's ex-husband.

"I'm going out now," I said. Celia came out of the kitchen. She was wearing one of my aprons, and she'd pulled her long, wavy brown hair into a ponytail.

"Please be gone for at least an hour," she said.

"Anything else I can do?"

"Yes, have a good time." I saluted her, and as I was leaving, I heard Jay say, "What record do you want to hear, Ceil?" Jay was in love with Celia. I knew it, he knew it, and, of course, Celia knew it.

9

I walked down the hill. The rain had finally stopped, and the air was damp with mist. I tried the mailbox again. A *Vogue* for Georgia, *Natural History* for Jay, and a white envelope for me with W. Jones printed above a New York City address. I slipped the magazines back in the box and put the letter in my pocket. I hurried in the opposite direction from town and turned right at the old back road. The sky was dark gray, and the air smelled richly of earth and rain.

I walked quickly until I came to my favorite spot by the pond. And then I sat down on an old log. My heart was pounding as I opened the letter.

Dear Kate,

Yesterday a girl came by the shop with eyes like yours. She had blond hair, too, but I think hers was dyed. She was looking for someone, I think. I don't know. But after she left I felt this terrible longing to see you, and nothing felt quite right for the rest of the day.

Happy birthday, Kate. I wish I could be there. I've enclosed this postcard I found at the Whitney Museum. I remembered how much you liked Edna St. Vincent Millay, and I thought this was such a pretty picture of her. I hope you do something wonderful on your birthday.

How are you doing? I can't believe it's been so long since I've seen you. How are Jay and Georgia? Send them my love.

So far I like it here all right. I miss the Berkshires, but the change is good for me. If you ever come to New York, I'll take you on the Staten Island Ferry. I'd like that. Would you?

Write to me, Kate. I miss you.

Love,
Will

I read the letter over again, and then I looked carefully at the postcard. It was a black-and-white photograph of Edna St. Vincent Millay standing by a magnolia tree. She looked lovely and tentative. On the back of the card Will had drawn a picture of a birthday cake with a black pen, and under the cake he'd written simply, "Sweet Sixteen."

I stuck the card back in the envelope, and then I read the letter again. *Will Jones.*

Will had curly brown hair, tortoiseshell glasses, and a slow, sexy smile. He had been Mattie's boyfriend for two years. They had loved each other a lot, but then Dean showed up, and after a while Mattie didn't want to see Will anymore. Will didn't take it very well. He was deeply in love with Mattie. Everyone knew that. And when she left with Dean, there was a look about Will, so desperate and lost, it made you want to turn away.

Will kept in touch with us, and once in a while he'd come over for dinner. Georgia had always loved Will. She thought he was kind and smart and gentle. He used to fix things around the house for us. He was a first-rate carpenter. He could make anything with his hands.

This year Will moved to New York City. He had a scholarship to study architecture. He'd written to me once in September and sent us all a card at Christmas. But I hadn't heard from him since, although I thought about him.

I loved Will. I loved him the whole time he and Mattie were going together. He used to call me his "Brown-eyed girl," from the Van Morrison song. I still loved him.

I put Will's letter away, and then I stood by the edge of the pond and threw stones in the water. I sang to myself. "Every time it rains, it rains pennies from heaven." It was an old song my mother used to sing to me. I threw the stones farther and farther out until my arm grew tired. The sky was charcoal now, and there was something about the trees and the water and the lushness after the rain that made me restless.

As I turned back toward home a red salamander shot out of my path, and I suddenly thought of a dream Mattie once had about a crocodile following her everywhere. It had frightened me so much, I was afraid I might have the same dream, but, of course, I never did. Mattie used to write her dreams down in a little black notebook. In another book, the composition kind, she wrote her poems. Six months after she'd gone, I found a grocery list in her old coat pocket, which said, "bananas, orange juice," and then, "Write about evening sky behind red farmhouse." For months and months after she'd gone there were traces of her everywhere.

Slowly I climbed the hill home. The light coming from the house was warm and yellow, and I knew Georgia was home because the Jeep was there. As I opened the front door I heard Georgia say, "She's back," and then she came running in and pulled me to her. "Happy birthday," she said, holding me tight. She lead me into the kitchen, which was decorated with crepe paper. There was a pile of presents on the kitchen table and a wonderful smell of roast chicken in the oven.

"Happy birthday!" Celia said, coming in from the living room. Jay followed close behind with his guitar, and then everyone was singing "Happy Birthday," and I started to cry.

There was a three-layer chocolate cake for dessert. And at midnight, when the sky cleared, we all went out to look at the moon.

CHAPTER TWO

I was dying to see Will. I thought about him all week long while I worked in Georgia's store. The whole time I was helping people pick out cotton sweaters or sachets of potpourri, I was thinking about what it would be like to see Will again.

Georgia's store was called Knit-Knacks. It used to be in Great Barrington, but then she moved it to West Stockbridge a few years ago. She sold handmade sweaters and rag dolls and bolts of calico and Liberty scarfs, and in the winter she sold antique Christmas decorations. The shop was small and narrow, and it smelled of lavender and lilac and straw. In the tiny back room there was a half-size refrigerator and a hot plate where a pot of coffee warmed all day long.

Twice a year Georgia and Vera, who did the book-

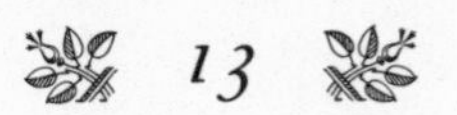

keeping for Knit-Knacks, would drive down South to pick up sweaters made by two sisters in Charleston. They would stop off at Vera's brother's house in South Carolina for a few days' rest before coming home.

The house always seemed quiet when Georgia was gone. She was a tall, large-boned woman with salt-and-pepper hair and an amazing laugh that went up in octaves depending on how funny something was to her. She was a terrible housekeeper and a worse cook. And she knew it.

"We're all pitching in," she'd say about cleaning and cooking. "It's the only way to make things bearable."

Jay and Mattie and I learned how to cook at an early age, and eventually we took over. The rare times Georgia did cook, we'd have macaroni and cheese for dinner, or chicken pot pie. She liked frozen foods and candy and the kind of hot chocolate that came out of a machine and tasted of powder. She thought nothing of having coffee and a piece of chocolate for breakfast.

"I believe sugar is good for the soul," she'd say.

She was my father's older sister and our only living relative. We went to live with her after our parents died. She was fifty years old and had been divorced for ten years when she took us in.

"This is your new home," she'd said about the old, red farmhouse in West Stockbridge. "Your new home." But, of course, we still thought of it as "Aunt Georgia's." It was a long time before we knew it as home.

The house was built in the early 1800s, and the rooms were small with low ceilings and wide-planked wooden floors. There was a fireplace in the kitchen, and Jay and I liked to do our homework at the kitchen table. In the living room there was an old velvet sofa that belonged to my grandmother. And above the sofa was a large oil painting by my mother. It was a self-portrait, and in the picture she was standing against a blue background, one long braid covering her right breast like a Tahitian girl. She wore a black dress that I vaguely remembered and long, silver earrings. The expression on her face was sad and a little severe, not at all the way I remembered my mother.

Georgia had loved my mother. My father was her little brother, fifteen years her junior, and she'd always felt protective of him.

"But when John met Nell, I knew he was a lucky man. In spite of how young they were when they met, there was something incredibly strong and wise about Nell."

In Georgia's store she'd hung two watercolors by my mother, which people often asked to buy. "Those aren't for sale," she'd say, smiling at me. "They're priceless."

Normally I liked working in the shop. I loved the

smell of potpourri and the feel of the soft cotton sweaters and the silky scarves. I liked working with Georgia and hearing her chat so openly with people, with strangers. But ever since I got the letter from Will I'd felt restive and lonely, unable to feel at home, either in the farmhouse or at the store. I'd spend hours staring at the maps on my walls, tracing imaginary routes from one country to another. I was longing to go someplace new. I was longing for something to happen.

In the early evenings, after supper, Georgia took a hot bath with a snifter of brandy. It was her quiet time to relax and ruminate. On Friday night Jay went out with some friends, and after doing the dishes, I wandered upstairs and knocked on the bathroom door.

"It's me," I said.

"Come in."

The bathroom was quite large and had a picture window that looked out onto the garden. It was great to take a hot, steamy bath in the winter and look out onto a field of snow. Now the room was moist with heat, and I felt my shirt cling to my back.

Georgia was lying back in the tub with one hand resting on her brandy glass. She wore a pink plastic shower cap.

"Nice hat," I told her.

"*Really*," she said. "They can send men to the moon, why can't they make a decent shower cap? Pass me that soap, please." I handed her a new bar of sea-mud soap and leaned against the sink.

"So, what's on your mind, dearie?" she asked.

"Well . . ."

"Yes?"

"Well, I've been thinking of going to see Will."

"Oh," she said, looking at me carefully. "How *is* Will?"

"He's pretty good."

"I'm glad."

"I was thinking of going with Jay. We both want to see him."

"I see." She took a sip of brandy and put the glass back on the flat edge of the tub. Her cheeks were flushed, and she looked pretty despite the shower cap.

"How long would you go for?"

"Just the weekend."

"And where would you stay?"

"With Will or Andy." Andy was an old friend of the family's who lived in Manhattan.

"When are you planning to go?"

"Next weekend?"

"It sounds like fun," she said.

"You don't sound very enthusiastic."

"It's not that. You know I love Will. It's just . . ."

"What?"

"Just be careful."

"Of *what*?"

"Don't expect too much."

18

"What do you mean?"

"Kate, I know you're very fond of Will, and he's fond of you." She paused for a moment, and then she spoke. "I don't want you to get hurt."

"How would I get hurt? It's not like *that*!" I said. "We're just old friends."

She looked at me, and I knew she knew how I really felt about Will.

"Don't expect too much," she said again softly.

I didn't say anything for a while, and then I said, "I don't expect anything, Georgia."

She looked into my eyes. "Why don't you have a chocolate? There's a new box by my bed."

"No thanks." I stood up. "So I can go with Jay to see Will?"

"I don't see why not," she said.

I leaned over and kissed her. "Thanks."

"*De nada.* That's Spanish," she said.

"No kidding."

"I think you should surprise Will," Celia said to me the next morning.

"But what if he's not planning to be in New York for the weekend? *That* would be some surprise."

It was crazy. Jay and I had talked about going to see Will, I'd even gotten permission from Georgia. The only person I hadn't told yet was Will. I liked the idea of surprising him.

19

"I could call up and say I might come in on Saturday, nothing definite. Then we'd know if he was going to be around," Jay suggested.

"Okay, but don't tell him I'm coming with you," I said. I was suddenly afraid Will was going to disappear.

CHAPTER THREE

It was all set. Jay and I would take the bus the following Friday morning and arrive in Manhattan by noon. All Will knew was that Jay might be coming to the city that weekend and would call him at work.

All week I was so excited, I could hardly sleep. I spent hours staring at myself in the mirror, trying new hairstyles. I'd put my hair up and then take it down and then put it up again.

"Georgia, do you think I should cut my hair?" I asked one night.

"How?"

"Short, I don't know."

"No, I think it's nice the way it is. You have beautiful hair."

"I'm not pretty, am I, Georgia?"

21

"I think you're better than pretty. You're interesting-looking." But she must have seen my dubious look. "You're not pretty in a conventional sense, but you have a real prettiness about you."

"How's that?"

"Well, you're tall and willowy and very feminine." I shook my head. "You're still growing into your looks, Kate."

"It's an awfully long wait," I told her.

At night I'd lie on my bed with only a candle to light the room. I'd stay up for hours listening to the radio, or sometimes I'd dance myself into a sweat. I sang a lot, too. And the whole time I was waiting to see Will, I felt my senses were keener, as if they had to be, as if I were standing on a precipice.

"Only a few more hours," I told myself on the day we were to leave. "A few more hours." What would he look like? The same? How much did people change? I hadn't seen Will in over a year. I was light with excitement, almost translucent. By the time Jay and I boarded the Greyhound bus, I felt as if I were taking off into space.

"The bus driver looks like Art Garfunkel," Jay whispered to me.

"No, he doesn't," I laughed. "Just the hair."

"*Just the hair!* What more do you need?"

"Ssh, he'll hear you."

"I'm hungry," Jay said.

"We just had breakfast."

"I know, but I'm always hungry after breakfast, aren't you?"

"No."

"I don't mean *right* after. I mean, say ten or fifteen minutes later."

"Sometimes," I said. "Let me look in my knapsack. I think Georgia threw something in before we left." I dug deep into my knapsack and felt a wax paper bag. "Doughnuts," I said, tossing the bag on his lap.

"I wonder if Georgia's going to miss us," he said, taking a bite of a chocolate doughnut.

"We're only going for two days."

"I know, but even if one of us goes away for a night, she seems so glad to see us when we come back. She should get married again," he said.

"You know how she feels about marriage."

"Well, then, she should have a boyfriend. She should go out. Why doesn't she go out?"

"I don't know. Maybe you stop wanting those things after a while." I crumpled up the paper bag and put it back in my knapsack. "Do you think she's ever sorry—you know, that she took us in? All that responsibility."

"What else could she have done? She had no choice."

"What do you mean? She could have not taken us. She could have said it was too much."

"And then what? Let us go to some foster home?"

23

"It happens," I said. "It happens all the time. Some people don't have enough money to take three kids, even if they want to. We were lucky."

"I know," he said. "I never said we weren't lucky."

I sat back and watched the bus driver turn the wheel in a great circular motion, as if he were churning butter. We drove through one town and then another and then out onto a ramp and onto the highway. Great dark clouds were forming in the sky, and I knew it was going to pour.

"We're on the road," Jay said, and I smiled.

When we were little, we'd stretch out on the living room floor and pore over a giant atlas. I longed to go to places with exotic or poetic names, like Singapore and the Ivory Coast and Aberystwyth.

Our parents had traveled a great deal before we were born. They took trains with Eurail passes and hitchhiked when their passes ran out. They went all over Europe and Great Britain and North Africa.

"It was the trip of trips," my mother used to say. "Enough memories to last a lifetime."

Jay and I had been infected by their talk of travel, by the photographs, by their excitement. That they had been young and spent four months on the open road appealed to our sense of romance and adventure.

"One day we'll all go on a long trip," my mother used to say. But there wasn't enough time.

Mattie and Jay and I grew up in a garden apartment of a red-brick house on West Eleventh Street. My father was an English professor at New York University, and my mother was a painter.

I loved our apartment. It was small and cozy, cluttered with books and paintings and worn, comfortable furniture. Jay and I shared a room with a dark green double-decker bed. Mattie's room was down the hall from ours. It was just big enough for a bed and bureau, and the walls were painted pale yellow. No one was allowed inside without her permission. There was a small kitchen with cream-colored walls and a living room that looked out onto a brick garden. My parents' room was off the living room. They had whitewashed walls and large windows, and the sunlight that poured inside was dazzling.

In the warmer months we would eat outside in the garden on a rickety round table. My mother would make cold, refreshing soups for dinner, borscht with dollops of sour cream in the center or gazpacho. On summer evenings she'd sit outside in her full white slip. She had thick, luxuriant hair, the color of wheat, and high, Slavic cheekbones. I thought she was so beautiful in her slip. Her skin was creamy and fragrant, and with her hair up in a bun, she looked to me like a ballerina getting ready for a performance.

My father was tall and boyishly handsome with great brown eyes and auburn hair. He adored my mother and she him. It was not that they didn't fight because they did, and, quite often, loudly. But there was a bond between them like an electric current, and you could *feel* their love for each other the way you could feel the heat of a summer day.

My parents met in 1957 in front of the Arts Student League where my mother was a student. Her name was Nell Voynow and at sixteen she looked like a woman of twenty. I have a picture of her then, wearing blue jeans and a beret, smiling brightly, the young bohemian artist. Her father, Jay, an American with Russian ancestors, died in World War II when she was a baby. She was raised by her mother, Sabrina, a Russian Jew from Kiev. They lived in Brooklyn, where Sabrina worked as a nurse, and moved to Manhattan when my mother was thirteen. At fifteen she graduated from high school and went to art school on a full scholarship.

My father grew up in Manhattan on East Twenty-first Street. His parents owned a small bookstore specializing in English literary works. His father, Nathanial Baker, was fifty-five when he was born; his mother, Anna, was forty-three.

"They were soft-spoken, bookish types," Georgia had told me. "They loved owning a bookstore, being surrounded by books." When they died, my father and Georgia divided some of the books among themselves and sold the rest.

My father was in graduate school when he met my mother. On their first date they went to Central Park, and he read her poems by his favorite poet and idol, Dylan Thomas. They sat on a big gray rock and ate ice cream and talked until it grew dark. A week later my mother brought my father home to meet her mother. My grandmother thought that they should wait a few years before they were married. But they were madly in love and didn't want to wait, couldn't wait. They were married at City Hall on my mother's seventeenth birthday. Mattie was born a year later.

"Will we go back to Eleventh Street?" I asked Jay.

"Sure, don't you want to?"

"Yes, I still dream about it."

"Me, too."

"I wonder if Mattie ever does."

"Who knows anything about Mattie?" Jay said.

The bus was picking up speed now, and I turned to look out the window. There's something about motion that jars the memory, takes the lid off so that people and places come tumbling out.

My mother wore silver earrings and silver rings. Her hands were long and slender and cool to touch. I wore one of her rings, a silver band with a deep blue, oval stone, a lapis lazuli. I remember my mother wearing this ring, the way it looked on her hand. It was as much a part of her as her own limbs, and wearing it made me feel close to her, as if she were still somehow a part of me.

My mother had her studio in the basement. It was wonderfully cool and dank, and it smelled of oil paints and turpentine. In the warmer months she'd set up her easel in the garden and work with watercolors. And when she wasn't painting, she drew constantly, mostly with charcoal on heavy white paper.

There was always music when she painted. Our house was full of music: Mozart, Bob Dylan, the Beatles. My mother especially loved Ray Charles. Sometimes, when we couldn't go to sleep at night, she'd sing to us whatever songs she'd been playing that day. And if that didn't work, she'd switch to Russian songs, the same ones her mother had sung to her when she, too, was a child afraid of the dark.

Outside it had begun to pour. An elderly man leaned forward and said to the bus driver, "It's raining cats and dogs, that's for sure." The bus driver didn't answer. I turned to my brother, but his eyes were closed. I sat very still as if in a trance as the bus sped along the cool, wet highway.

CHAPTER FOUR

I was not prepared for the heat; it was almost tropical. The air was heavy with humidity, and it was cloying and oppressive.

"New York in the summer," Jay said.

"I had forgotten." I had forgotten all the people and the constant sounds of traffic, and my senses felt vulnerable and bombarded, as if someone had suddenly turned up the volume too high on a stereo.

It was a gray, glaring day, the kind of light that made colors look that much brighter. The yellow of a taxicab, the red wash of a building, the dark green of a leaf. We had taken the train to Spring Street, and now we were unsure of which direction to go.

"Excuse me," Jay said to a young man with black sunglasses.

"We're looking for Soho."

"You're in it," he said.

"Oh. Where's Broome Street?"

"About five blocks up that way."

"Thanks."

Soho was full of art galleries and restaurants and expensive-looking boutiques. Yet, despite all the activity of trucks unloading and people shopping, there was a grayness about the area, due to the industrial buildings, the lack of trees, and the seeming lack of sky.

We were only a few blocks from the shop where Will worked as a cabinetmaker, and we tried to hurry.

"I hope he'll be glad to see us," I said.

"Of course he'll be. You worry too much, Kate."

The shop was a long, narrow storefront with a high ceiling. It had the sweet, fruity smell of wood shavings and a light film of sawdust hung in the air. The floor was blond wood, and it was full of deep scratches and crevices, as if someone had taken a knife and carved in it. Screwdrivers and levels were hung neatly along a wall, and slabs of plywood were stacked against another. There were worktables with wheels and benches with blue vices, and in one corner there was a table saw where a small man was sawing a piece of wood.

Will stood with his back to us. He wore a pair of green headphones and was busy marking lines on a piece of wood with a square. Somewhere a radio played opera. The high-pitched wail of the saw rose into the air and then stopped. Will drew some more lines, tapped his pencil against the table, and then turned around. His mouth dropped open. As if in slow motion, I watched a smile creep across his face. He ripped off his headphones.

"What are you guys doing here?" he said, but before we could answer, he was running over and throwing his arms around us, pulling us close in his embrace. He smelled of sweat and Old Spice, of comfort. My eyes stung with tears.

"What a great surprise," he said, looking at me, and then we all started smiling and laughing and I was giddy with relief.

"You guys been camping?" he said, noting our knapsacks.

"Yes, in the wilds of Central Park," Jay said.

"Seriously, what are you doing here? I thought you were going to call me," he said to Jay.

"We wanted to surprise you," I said. "Surprise!"

"This is too much. Did you get my birthday letter, Kate?"

"On the day itself."

"I'm glad." He took a few steps back to look at us. "You're all grown-up," he said, staring at me.

"Well, these things happen," I said a little nervously, and he laughed.

Will took us to his favorite coffee shop. There was a long counter on one wall and booths along the other. As we were walking to the back a redheaded waitress passed by and said, "Hi there, Will."

"Hello, Francine," he said. "That's Mean Francine," he whispered in my ear. "It took me six months to get her to smile. Now she loves me." As soon as we sat down Francine came by and plopped down three menus. "Be right back," she said.

"Best cheeseburgers in the country," Will said. "Best BLTs and second-best apple pie. The first being yours, Kate." I smiled. I used to make apple pie for Will with the secret hope that he would fall in love with me.

"We were going to call," said Jay, "but then we decided to go for broke. We figured the worst that could happen was that you'd pretend you didn't know us."

"Are you kidding? I'm thrilled to see you. You're going to stay with me, aren't you?"

"Well, we already called Andy, and he's expecting us sometime today."

"So call him up and say there's been a change of plans. You can't come all the way to New York to surprise me and then not stay with me. And, wait till you see where I'm staying."

"I don't think Andy would mind," I said. Will smiled at me and I smiled back. I felt my heart beat faster. It was so good to see him again.

I sat back and listened as Jay and Will talked about colleges and Jay's plans to study medicine one day. It was like old times when the three of us would sit around the kitchen table at Georgia's and talk late into the night. Will had always been easy to talk to. He had a way of making you feel safe and comfortable. He was good at bringing people out of themselves. Even Mattie opened up when she was with Will. I remember the first time she told me about him.

"Oh, Kay, I've met the most fantastic boy."

"Who is he? What's his name?"

"Will. William Jones. Oh, wait till you see him. You'll really like him. Look what he gave me." She'd opened her gray velvet bag and taken out her diary. Pressed flat between some pages was a pink rose. "He said my skin was like roses, can you imagine?" I had been fascinated and sick at the same time. I had not even met Will, and already I wanted him for myself. Wanted someone like him, wanted romance, longed for romance. At ten I thought that falling in love was one of the greatest things that could happen to you.

"We can talk about *everything*," she'd said, "like old friends." And I'd wondered desperately what it was that they talked about.

The first time I met Will, he'd reached out his hand and said, "Pleased to meet you, Katharine." I was only ten and he was sixteen, and I didn't know older boys could be so gallant. Georgia invited him to stay for supper, and I sat in almost total silence, watching the graceful manner in which he carried himself, the ease with which he conversed with Jay and Georgia. Nor did I miss for one second the way he and Mattie smiled at one another. I'd never seen her so animated.

"He's very nice, your friend Will," Georgia told her later.

"Isn't he?" Mattie said, and then, in a rare mood of affection, I saw her fling her arms around Georgia's neck.

"I'm so glad you like him," she said, kissing her cheek. "So glad." And then she turned and ran upstairs to her room.

"I think someone is falling in love," Georgia said, turning to me with a wink.

"Who?" I said angrily, knowing perfectly well who she meant.

"Don't worry, dearie," she said, slipping her arm around me. "Your time will come. You've got plenty of time for all that."

A few weeks after she met him Will gave Mattie a wooden box he'd made out of cherry wood. It was six inches long and four inches wide and there was a little brass hook to loop through a brass ring when she wanted to close it.

I remember Will showed it to me before he gave it to Mattie.

"What do you think, Katharine? Think she'll like it?" I ran my fingers gently across the smooth, lovely wood.

"It's beautiful, Will."

"You really think so?" I nodded. "Look what's inside," he said. I carefully opened the box. Engraved on the bottom in delicate, script letters were Mattie's initials, M.S.B.

"Did you do that, too?" I asked.

"Yes, it's not hard."

I closed the box and handed it back to Will.

"A hit or a miss?" he said.

"Oh, definitely a hit."

"Hope you're right," he said, patting my shoulder.

But I was right. Mattie loved the cherry-wood box. It was one of the few things she took with her when she ran away with Dean.

CHAPTER FIVE

After lunch Will went back to work, and Jay and I went to see Andy. We walked through Washington Square Park, the park where I'd learned how to ride a bike, all in an afternoon. I was six years old at the time, and I would not let my father help me but insisted on doing it myself, and by the end of the day, I was riding alongside Jay, standing up and waving triumphantly to my father.

The grass smelled soggy, the same as I remembered. And for a moment the scent was intoxicating and I felt my childhood clutch at me.

Andy lived in a two-bedroom apartment on East Ninth Street, just off University Place. It was a pretty, old, rent-controlled building, and he'd lived there for twenty years. The hallways were cool with high ceilings, and the elevator had dark wood walls and a wooden bench to sit on.

"Well, well, come in, come in," Andy said to us. We hadn't seen him in almost a year, not since he'd come to spend Thanksgiving with us at the farmhouse. He kissed us both heartily, and then he folded his arms in front of his chest and shook his head.

"You've both grown so much. How tall are you, Jay?"

"Six-two."

"Six-two! You look seven feet." My brother was handsome with dark blond hair that was always falling in his eyes. He was tall like our father, but he had a thin, wiry strength of his own.

"Well, we'll have to take out the measuring tape later." Andy loved to measure us. Georgia said he thought of Jay and Mattie and me as his nieces and nephew.

"Kate, you've got your mother's lovely hair," he said, patting my head. "Don't ever cut it."

"I won't."

"Now come in and tell me everything. You must be thirsty. I have some iced tea made with fresh mint. How does that sound?"

"Great."

"Sit, sit," he told us, and he hurried into the kitchen.

Andy's apartment hadn't changed in all the years

I'd known him. The living room was sunny and crowded with plants and flowers and a vast collection of glass bottles. Framed theater posters covered the walls. Andy had been an actor as a young man and later a playwright. He was sixty now and balding. He had a warm, friendly smile.

I walked around the apartment. In the hallway between the bedroom and the living room was a large oil painting my mother did of Andy as a young man. There was an abstract feel to the painting. Bold strokes, lots of red and yellow, Andy's features implied rather than clearly drawn.

"She improvised, really," he once told me. "After all, she never knew me as a young man, I was middle-aged when we met. This was how she imagined me as a youth," he'd said. "What a lovely imagination she had."

As I walked around, a sleek, black cat called Ophelia followed at my heels. Andy loved cats. At present he had three: Ophelia; Henry the Fifth, a fat, gray long-haired; and King Lear, a small pretty tiger who looked more like a kitten than a cat. When I came back in the living room, King Lear was rubbing his head against Jay's legs.

"King Lear! Behave yourself!" Andy said, coming in with a tray. He passed us each a tall glass of tea. "Help yourselves to sugar," he said, pushing the sugar bowl toward us.

38

"Now, are you sure you'll be all right staying with Will?" he said. Jay had called Andy from the coffee shop and told him our new plans.

"Yes, fine," Jay said.

"Well, you have a key to here, just in case. And if you change your mind, you know you're always welcome."

"Thanks, Andy," I said. I moved to sit on the edge of his armchair. The apartment was almost chilly, and I remembered Andy hated hot weather.

"Tell me all the gossip," he said, patting my back. "How is the store?"

"It's doing well," I said.

"How's Georgia holding up?"

"She's fine," said Jay. "Why don't you come and see us?"

"Oh, I'll wait till the fall. Can't stand the mosquitoes. I'll come in November and then we'll do another Thanksgiving. Remember that sumptuous pumpkin pie I bought and how I tried to convince Georgia I'd baked it myself?"

"She never believed you," I said, laughing.

"I suppose not. So what have you kids been up to?" he asked. "Playing any basketball, Jay?"

Jay had played basketball all through high school, where his teammates named him "Smooth." He was beautiful to watch in action. He had a way of gliding while other players ran. He never seemed to lose his composure, and while he was quick, he gave the impression of moving in slow motion. Often I used to find him moving around the house, engaged in a pantomime game, dodging invisible opponents and dribbling a nonexistent ball.

"I haven't played much this summer," Jay said. "I pick up a game once in a while."

"What's new on the college front?"

"I've decided to take a year off and then go to U. Mass the following September."

"Still planning to study premed?"

"Yes."

"Good! Every family should have a doctor in it. And I'm all for this taking a year off. It's a good idea."

"Well, I've saved up money, and I want to take a trip cross-country."

"Yes, see the desert and the mountains, absolutely! It's a great trip."

"Then I'll work some more and go to Europe in the spring."

"Europe, of course! You must go straight to Paris. It's extraordinary—the light is completely different over there. And the food, *Mon Dieu*, you can live on the bread and coffee alone. And the museums! You'll lose yourself in the *Jeu de Paume* and find yourself a changed man." Jay and I smiled at each other.

"What about you, Angel?" Andy said to me. "You have one more year of school, right?"

"Right."

"And then?"

"I don't know, Andy." I felt very vague about college. "I'd like to travel, like Jay, but I don't really know what I want to do after that."

"Well, there's no rush, is there? You've got plenty of time to figure it all out." He smiled at me. "Still like to sing?"

"Yes," I said shyly. I used to sing for Andy when I was little.

"Good, good! Any news from Mattie?" I looked at Jay, and he looked at me. The room suddenly felt ten degrees cooler.

"No news," I said quietly.

He shook his head sadly. "What a pity. These family chasms could tear your heart out."

"What's a chasm?" I asked.

"A cleft in the earth, a separation." It was true, when Mattie ran away she left a hole as wide and as deep as the Grand Canyon.

"She's an interesting girl, Mattie," Andy said. "You never knew what she was thinking. I only met Dean once, but I thought he was just a phase she was going through. The handsome man on a motorcycle, the modern romance. He rode up on his Triumph instead of on a white horse. I used to tell Georgia not to worry so much, that we'd all picked the wrong people at some point in our lives, and it would eventually work out. I never thought Mattie would run away with him."

"You didn't know her," I said.

"No, I guess not. She should have stayed with Will," he said. "Will loved her with a Romeo-like passion."

I stood up suddenly.

"How is Will?" Andy asked.

I let Jay answer and excused myself and went to the bathroom.

I washed my face and hands. I took out my tortoise-shell comb and ran it through my hair, and then I swept my hair back off my left temple and slipped the comb in place. Andy didn't know better, but still, he'd wounded me, and for a moment I hated him.

When I came back to the living room, Andy was talking about a play he was writing.

"It's going to be done up at Provincetown next year, if I ever finish the rewrites."

I looked at Jay, and he knew what I was thinking.

"We should go, Andy," he said. "We told Will we were going to pick him up at work and we want to walk around a bit first."

"Wait, before you go, I have something for you." Andy went into the bedroom and came back with an envelope.

"I thought you might like to have this," he said.

42

When I opened the envelope, there was a photograph inside.

It was a picture of my parents. I knew it had been taken before they were married because the date stamped on the white edge of the photograph said 1957. They were sitting on a park bench in Central Park. My father was facing the camera with an amused smile on his face; he had one arm around my mother. She was looking off to the side with a surprised expression, as if something had just caught her attention. They both looked so young. I don't think I'd ever seen them look so young.

"Oh, Andy."

"I was rummaging through some old boxes and I found it," he said.

"Did you take the picture?" Jay asked.

"Yes. I remember it was in the spring and we'd just had a picnic in the park. Your parents had told me they were going to be married. I was so happy for them. We were all very happy that day." We stood there, quietly staring at the photograph. The room was silent except for the humming of the air conditioner.

There is something terrible about seeing a picture of your parents when they were young. The shock of recognition that perhaps, after all, they were not so different from you. To see them as people separate from you, to see them way before you were even born, before they became a mother or father, before their lives were changed forever and yours began.

"Anyway, I wanted you to have this," Andy said.

"Thank you," I whispered.

"I was always a bit in love with your mother, you know," he said softly. "You remind me so much of her, Kate." I took the photograph and put it carefully back in the envelope. "Wait there's something else," Andy said. He disappeared again and returned with two packages.

"*Pour mademoiselle*," he said, handing me one. "*Et monsieur*." I unwrapped a bottle of perfume, Diorissimo. It had a light, flowing scent.

"Thank you, I don't have any perfume," I told him. I kissed his cheek, and he held me close.

"You are my children," he whispered hoarsely. "You know that."

"Oh, Andy."

He took the perfume from me and dabbed some behind my ears and on my wrists. "Pulse spots," he said. "Mm, divine, it suits you."

Jay's present was a book of short stories by Chekov.

"You haven't read these, have you?"

"No," said Jay.

"I remembered you liked short stories, and these are very good. Every young person should read Chekov."

"Thanks, Andy."

"Now, call me if you need anything—and have a

wonderful time. Oh, and give my best to Will."

Jay and I were silent going down in the elevator. When we got outside, Jay looked at me and said, "Eleventh Street?" I nodded. And then, with great excitement and not a little trepidation, we headed for home.

CHAPTER SIX

The house hadn't changed that much. The present tenants had put white geraniums in the upstairs windows, and they looked very pretty. The front steps were the same, that New York putty color. Pink putty, really. I loved those steps. To the right of the stairs was a black iron gate with an Egyptian-like pattern on the lower half. Once you opened the gate you walked down two steps to the door of our old apartment. Of course, we didn't open the gate now, we just looked.

Across the street was the New School, and down the block from that was Gene's, an Italian restaurant where my parents had taken me for my eighth birthday.

"Let's go to the graveyard," I said to Jay. We walked past our house toward the end of the block. There was a tiny graveyard set off from the street by an iron gate. A sign I'd never noticed before read, THE SECOND CEMETERY FOR THE SPANISH AND PORTUGUESE SYNAGOGUE SHEARITH ISRAEL, IN THE CITY OF NEW YORK, 1805–1829."

"I never knew that," I said to Jay.

"I didn't, either."

There were only a few headstones, faded a ghostly white amid the lush green ferns and tangled ivy. Once, when we were little, there was a huge snowstorm, and Mattie and Jay and I had played in this cemetery, pretending it was a castle. The iron gate was open then, and the snowstorm had covered all the graves. We'd played inside here for hours, until our mother came to get us. Now the gate was locked, probably to keep out vagrants.

We walked back to our house and stood there staring at the front stoop. It was here where Mattie and Jay and I would wait for our father to come home from work. We'd spot him at the end of the block, coming from Fifth Avenue, and we'd leap to our feet and tear off down the street yelling, "Daddy, Daddy!"

"What a reception," he'd say. "You'll frighten the neighbors." But he'd pick each of us up and kiss us warmly.

"How are you kids doing?"

"Fine, Daddy."

"Good, Daddy."

"And how's your mother?"

"She's fine."

"You *always* ask that, Daddy."

"Well, I always want to know."

On the weekends he'd take us to Washington Square Park so our mother could have time to paint. He'd sit casually on a bench, reading or grading papers, looking up every now and then to make sure we were still there. He wore his weekend clothes: faded jeans, a workshirt, and sneakers.

"Watch me, Daddy, watch me!" I'd say as I hung upside down from the jungle gym.

"That's good, Katie," he'd say with a smile, and then he'd go back to his work.

Sometimes on the way home, if he were in a good mood, he'd break into a soft shoe in the middle of the sidewalk.

"Daddy, don't, please," we'd say, laughing with embarrassment, which only egged him on.

"I'm singing in the rain," he'd sing.

"Dad, Dad," we'd say, pulling on his pant legs. "Come on, stop!"

"Do I know you?" he'd ask, which would make us fall over, shrieking with laughter, half at his being so ridiculous and half with fear because what if he really didn't remember us—then what would happen?

The air was getting cooler now, and the light was no longer harsh but pale and opal. I wondered what my father would look like if he were alive today, but of course, I couldn't imagine. My parents would always be frozen in time, remaining the way I remembered them as a child. My brain a wall of photographs and images.

"I thought I'd feel better seeing the house," Jay said, "but I don't. Do you?"

"I don't know." We'd been to the city a few times since our parents died, but we had never come back to this house. I think we'd been afraid.

"It's weird, isn't it?" he said. His eyes were glassy. I moved closer to him and put my hand on his arm. He had always protected me when we were small, held my hand when we crossed the street, beaten up kids who bullied me. And then, when our parents died and everything was blown into infinitesmal pieces, he still tried to protect me. He would never leave me the way Mattie had. Our hearts were as rooted and entwined as the tangled green of the graveyard.

We walked for a few blocks in silence, and then Jay said, "I always think that if they hadn't gone to that party, if it hadn't rained that night, if they had not taken that road or borrowed that car, they'd still be here."

"It will never make any sense," I said.

Georgia had been with us the night it happened. The next morning she told us they had been killed in an automobile crash, that they had died instantly. The word *instantly* confused me, and for a long time afterward I thought it meant that they had evaporated on the spot, vanished into the cold winter evening. For a long time afterward I did not believe they were dead.

49

"You used to think they were coming back," Jay said.

"So did you."

"Remember, you thought they were waiting to surprise you on your birthday."

"I remember."

"You told me they were only *pretending* to be dead."

"Oh, I had such high hopes," I said sadly.

We kept walking.

CHAPTER SEVEN

Will was staying on the top floor of what used to be an old warehouse on West Twenty-eighth Street. He was subletting it for the summer, rent-free in return for some carpentry work.

"There's no air conditioning, but the fans work pretty well," he said. "Come on, I'll give you the grand tour."

It was an enormous loft with high ceilings and a wall of porthole windows overlooking the street. The floors were painted battleship gray, and they were slightly warped and uneven in places, so that when you walked, you could feel a tilt beneath you as if you were truly out on the open sea.

"Why, you live in a ship," I said, and Will laughed.

The place was sparse. An old couch here, a table

there. Records and books were stacked against a wall in cartons.

"You can sleep here, Kate," he said, leading us behind a thin wooden partition. There was a bed with striped sheets, and next to the bed was an orange crate filled with books.

"Is this your room?"

"Yes, but I want you to have it. It's the most private. Jay and I can sleep in the living room."

"Are you sure, because I don't mind—"

"Please, I insist."

"Well, thank you."

We went into the kitchen, and I opened the refrigerator. There was a carton of milk and an old bag of granola.

"Hmm, a hearty sight," I said.

"Damn, I was sure I had more stuff."

"It's okay."

"No, let me go down and get some things for dinner. What do we want to eat?"

"Chinese food," Jay and I said at the same time.

"Well, that was easy," said Will.

We ate Chinese food straight out of the white cartons, and I drank cold ginger ale and Will and Jay drank beer. Later we called Georgia, and Will got on the phone and they had a nice chat.

"She's great, your Aunt Georgia," he said.

"The best of the best," said Jay.

52

We stayed up till midnight, talking and listening to music. Will said he was going to take us to a big party on Saturday night.

"I don't have anything to wear," I said.

"You can wear what you've got on," he told me. "Don't worry about it."

When it was time to go to bed, it was hard to fall asleep, knowing Will was so close in the dark. I kept closing my eyes and then opening them. The darkness had a silver graininess to it. It felt alive. I got up to get a glass of water.

"Kate?" I turned and could just make out Will moving toward me.

"Can't you sleep?" he asked.

"No."

"I can't, either. Come here." He fumbled for my hand in the dark. We climbed out onto the fire escape. There was a breeze, and it was cooler than it had been all day.

"It's nice out here," I said. The sky was purple-black, and there was a view of water towers and rooftops across the street. "You could use some plants out here, though."

"I could use a lot of things," he said. "So what have you been up to these days, Katarina?"

"Oh, I don't know. I think sometimes that I want to be a singer."

"You should! I love your voice. It's very sexy."

"Oh, Will," I said, looking away. "What about you?"

"Oh, I don't think I should sing." I hit him gently on the arm, and he took my hand in his.

"You've gotten so pretty, Kate."

"Thanks, but you don't have to say that."

"I wouldn't say it if I didn't mean it. I think you're very pretty."

"You're pretty, too," I said, and he laughed. "Hey, I just realized you quit smoking."

"I was waiting for you to notice."

"How long has it been?"

"Almost eight months."

"Do you miss it?"

"Sometimes. For example, this would be a perfect time for a cigarette."

"Well, I'm proud of you."

"Thank you, my dear." He was staring at me again, and I had the feeling he wanted to tell me something. Neither of us said anything for a while, and then Will spoke.

"So, do you have a boyfriend—back home, as they say."

"I don't know, not really."

"What does, 'not really' mean?"

"I guess it means no."

"I'm sure lots of boys must be falling all over you."

"Why do you say that?"

"I can tell."

"I think you've gotten a little crazy in your old age, Will."

"You do?"

"Yup."

"Well, maybe you're right." He smiled at me. His face was very pale in the half-lit darkness. He took off his glasses and rubbed his eyes. There were little lines under them and shadows I'd never seen before.

"I think I'll go to sleep now," I said. I stood up and started to climb back in the window.

"Kate?" I turned around. "I'm glad you came."

"Me, too. 'Night, Will."

" 'Night."

The next morning while Will was sleeping Jay and I went out and bought groceries. When Will woke up, I fixed us all a big breakfast of French toast with blueberries and syrup.

"I never get to eat like this," Will said. And for a moment I wished I lived with him in the ship on Twenty-eighth Street and that we could eat big breakfasts together and stay up late at night listening to music or talking out on the fire escape.

After breakfast Will wanted to show us the Flatiron building on Twenty-third Street, and then we walked downtown into the East Village.

"The East Village has become very popular," said Will. "You can still buy an apartment here for cheap if you're willing to fix it up. There are some great-looking buildings down here."

We walked down St. Mark's Place. There were punks everywhere and people roller-skating. A pretty, black woman walked by me with an Afro the color of cotton candy. Unlike Soho, the East Village was gritty and full of color. I found a shop that sold silver jewelry and dragged Will and Jay inside. Pavarotti was singing on the radio, and his great, booming voice filled the room. The air smelled of cigarette smoke.

I looked in the glass case at rows and rows of earrings. "I like those," I said to Will, pointing to a pair of thin silver hoops.

"They would look nice on you," he said.

"Hey, Kate," called Jay from the back of the store. "Do you think Celia would like this?" He held up a silver chain. I went over to look at it. It was very delicate, and I tried it on so Jay could see how it looked.

"I think she'll love it," I said.

"Good," he said. "Then I'll buy it."

"And it's a good price," said the saleslady. "A very good price." Jay asked her to put it in a box. When we went to the front of the store, Will was gone. I looked outside and there he was, beckoning to me.

"What's the matter?" I said.

"Nothing, the smoke was getting to me. Do you mind if we keep walking?"

"No, but do you mind if I keep shopping? I want to buy a dress."

"No, of course I don't mind."

I found just the dress I wanted. It was a dancer's dress, made of a wonderful material that you never have to iron. It was a dusty rose color, sleeveless like a tunic. And when I put it on, it made me think of Isadora Duncan dancing under the Acropolis.

We spent the rest of the day walking around the city. I bought a cream-colored straw bag for Georgia and a long, printed scarf for Celia. Before going uptown Will took us to a small Polish coffee shop on First Avenue, and we all shared a plate of cherry blinis with sour cream.

About an hour before the party I took a long shower, turning the faucets slowly from hot to cold. While I was still damp I dabbed some of the perfume Andy gave me behind my ears and on the insides of my wrists. I slipped on my new dress and wrapped my hair into a low bun at the base of my neck.

I was cool after the shower. And there was something in the air, in the perfume, in the softness of the summer night that made me feel all at once that I was beautiful.

I stepped into the living room.

"*Qué linda*," said Will. I blushed. "I have something for you," he said, handing me a small box. Inside were the silver hoop earrings.

"Will!"

"I had to buy them quickly, when your back was turned. And then I had to hurry you out of there before you went ahead and bought them yourself." I went over and kissed him on the cheek. I took out my old earrings and slipped in the hoops.

"How do they look?"

"Great. You're the silver girl, Kate."

"I guess I am."

The party was in a loft on Prince Street. We had to climb five flights of long, steep stairs, and the hallway smelled of must and plaster. I could tell when we were getting nearer because the music was growing louder.

"Oh, hi, Will," said a woman standing by the door. She was in her late twenties with short black hair and a green rubber necklace that glowed in the dark.

"Hi, Leslie," he said, kissing her cheek. He introduced us, and Leslie told us to make ourselves at home. "There's plenty of food and beer, so help yourselves."

The place was dimly lit and packed with people, and the music was so loud you could feel it pulsating under your feet. The smell of marijuana hung in the air like mist.

"Come on," Will said, taking my hand. I followed him through the crowd into a small kitchen area. There was an aluminum tub filled with ice and beer, and on a counter were trays of cheese and crackers and dips and an ice bucket filled with strawberries.

Will handed me and Jay a beer, and then we found a place next to a wall where we could watch people dancing. "I wish Celia were here," Jay whispered to me. A girl in a shiny paper jumpsuit came over to talk to Will.

"This is Jolie," he said. I smiled, but Jolie looked right over my head and turned back to Will. Her eyes were made up with blue and green and magenta eye shadow, and I thought she looked like a parrot. She asked Will where he'd been lately, and he said simply, "Around." Buddy Holly's "That'll Be the Day" came on.

"Let's dance," Will said, taking my hand.

I love to dance. I hardly ever got a chance because I didn't go to many parties, but I'd dance up a storm alone in my room or sometimes with Jay around the house.

We danced without touching, but the floor was so crowded, people kept knocking into us. After Buddy Holly, Martha and the Vandellas' "Heat Wave" came on, and people went wild. Most of the music being played was from the fifties and sixties. We danced until my neck and back were damp with sweat, and I felt my dress cling to me.

When at last a slow song came on, Will put his arms around me and drew me close.

"You have such beautiful eyes," he whispered. "Do you know that?" I shook my head. His breath was warm against my neck. I wanted to kiss him, to tell him that I loved him, but I did not have the courage.

"Are you having a good time, Kate?"

"Oh, yes!"

"Me, too." We danced in a slow circle, taking little,

uncertain steps, like people who were drunk, except we weren't.

We danced to two more songs after that, and then Will said it was time to leave. I was half sorry, but by then I was too tired to protest, and I fell asleep in the taxi with the pale sensation of Will's arms wrapped around me.

Sunday we all slept late into the day, and in the afternoon Jay went to the Museum of Natural History with Andy and Will, and I went to Battery Park. At sunset we boarded the ferry for Staten Island. It was an old boat made of wood, and it seemed incredibly solid and trustworthy. The breeze from the river was full of spray, and I was glad to be out on the water.

We hardly spoke on the way to Staten Island, but coming back, Will broke the silence.

"I had a really nice time with you, Kate."

"Me, too."

"I wish . . ."

"What?"

"Nothing, I . . . You know, you're not anything like Mattie." My heart changed rhythm and I moved away from him.

"I don't mean it's bad . . . it's good. You're your own self."

"I don't know if I am or not. I really don't know."

We didn't say anything for a while. I shook off my

scarf and let my hair go loose in the wind. The sky had turned mauve around us. He turned to me.

"It's been four years and I still dream about her. I walk by your old house and imagine her there as a kid. Anything that's connected to her is important."

"Like me?" The pain was sharp, and I waited for it to go away.

"You're her sister. I can't separate you from that. But you know I've always loved you, always thought our friendship was special."

He was right, and still the word *friendship* wrung my heart. I remembered what Georgia once said about being in love with the wrong man, how it happens to all of us.

I leaned into the rail. "I thought you might be in love with *me*," I said. "Pretty silly of me, eh?"

"Oh, Kate," he said, slipping his arm around me. We stayed like that until we reached Manhattan.

CHAPTER EIGHT

"Do you want to tell me what happened in New York?" Georgia asked me as we were driving home from Knit-Knacks one evening.

"Nothing happened."

"Kate, you've been crying all week. Something must have happened."

"*Nothing* happened. I just hate myself, that's all."

Georgia pulled the car off the road, and we came to a slow stop.

"Now listen to me. Whatever happened with you and Will is no reason to hate yourself. Women are always doing that," she said angrily.

"What?"

"Hating themselves."

I didn't answer.

"He's not the only man in the world."

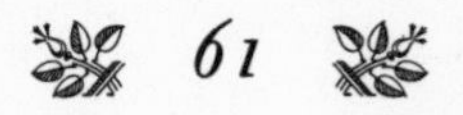

"For me he is."

"You're too young to say that."

"I can't help what I feel, can I?"

"What happened?"

I shook my head. "He still loves Mattie."

"Well, that's his choice you know, Kate."

"I don't think he can help it." It didn't matter how long Mattie had been gone or even that she was married. He loved her. He would always love her.

"Well, whatever Will thinks of Mattie doesn't really have anything to do with you, does it? It's between them. When it comes to men, you have to put a little chicken fat around your heart. Believe me, I know how it can hurt."

"I don't know . . . I . . ."

"Listen to me, darling girl. You're going to meet lots of men in your life, and you know what I want you to do?"

"What?"

"I want you to line them all up like asparagus and take your pick."

I smiled. "I love you, Georgia."

"I love you, too, Cookie."

August came. Jay worked full-time at a pharmacy in Great Barrington. He was still planning to go cross-country in September. Business was good in Georgia's store, and Celia came three days a week to help out.

There was something different about Celia. We

were still close, but I noticed that she and Jay were spending more and more time together. And when she came to visit, instead of coming into my room first, she went to see Jay.

"Are you in love with Jay?" I asked her one night.

"I'm not sure. Would you mind if I was?"

"Of course not," I lied. But I was afraid I might lose her to Jay. We were sitting in her room, putting on makeup. Celia was painting my nails with a deep red lacquer.

"I don't know why they call this Valentine. It should be called Blood."

"I don't think that would sell, do you?"

"You never know."

"Now wait for it to dry, Kate," she said. "You never let it dry properly." I blew on my nails, one at a time. Celia took a scissors and started snipping off her split ends.

"My father called," she said. "He wants me to spend the last three weeks of August with him."

"Are you going to?"

"I'm not sure. I don't know if I want to leave the Berkshires." She's in love with Jay, I thought.

I leaned into her mirror and applied a red lipstick that was so dark, it was almost black. The night was warm and I felt restless.

"Let's do something," I said.

"There's a concert in Tanglewood," she said.

"Let's go."

64

We brought a picnic supper of cucumber sandwiches and lemon cake. Jay met us there. A country-and-western band I'd never heard of was playing, and they sang a lot of Willie Nelson songs. We ate the sandwiches and drank ice-cold milk with the cake, and later, as it grew dark, we lay back on the blanket and stared up into the sky. It was a balmy evening. The stars were scattered through the sky like points of light on a gigantic map. The music mingled with the sounds of a summer night, with the hushed voices of people whispering, with a baby crying in the distance. I lay on my back with my hands folded behind my head.

"Now, this is the life," Celia said. She was lying on her side. Her long hair was loose down her back. The silver chain Jay had bought her glimmered in the dark.

"I wish we could sleep here," she said.

"We can," Jay murmured.

"No, we can't; not really."

I closed my eyes and listened to the music. I thought about Will and felt a stab in my heart, a reflex reaction. I let out a sigh.

"Kate?"

"What?"

"Forget about him."

"I'm trying."

"I know." Her breath smelled sweet, of bubble gum.

"Have any more gum, Ceil?"

"Just this," she said, pointing to her mouth. "Want half?"

"Sure." She pulled out part of her gum and gave it to me.

"I wish I could meet someone. I wish it had been different with Will." *I wish I weren't so lonely.* Celia reached out and took my hand. "If only I were beautiful and dazzling."

"To me you are," she said.

I smiled. "That's just 'cause you love me."

She shook her head.

"You know what the worst part is?"

"What?"

"The whole time he sent me the letter and gave me the earrings and we danced at that party I told you about and I was wearing my new dress—that *whole time* he was still in love with Mattie."

"Forget about him, Kate. I mean it." She looked at me closely. "You know what your problem is?"

I shook my head.

"You don't give up easily."

"No," I said. "No, I don't."

CHAPTER NINE

"You got a package," Jay told me. He was picking me up from work, as Georgia was driving to Vera's that night for dinner.

"From who?"

"From Mattie." I stared at him.

"Are you kidding?" He stopped at a red light and turned to me.

"Hardly," he said.

"Where is it?"

"It's back at the house."

"Where is it from?"

"Nova Scotia."

"Nova Scotia! What's she doing there?"

"How would I know?"

"I wonder why she's sending me a package."

"For your birthday, I guess. She's only a few years

late." I watched him push his hair roughly out of his face.

"You can see for yourself," he said as we pulled up in front of the house. I stared at my brother. He had our mother's violet eyes. They were unimaginably beautiful. The sun was setting, and an orange light streamed into the car. We both sat still for a moment after he turned off the motor, and then suddenly I pushed open the door and ran inside.

It was a large, square package wrapped in brown wrapping paper. The sight of the familiar handwriting made my heart jump as if I'd missed a step going down a flight of stairs. I ripped the paper carefully and took out a white cardboard box, which was slightly crushed along the edges. Inside the box was a chamois jacket with fringes down the front, Davy Crockett-style. It was the color of butter and wheat, and the inside had a silk lining. It was the softest thing I'd ever felt, and when I held it up to me, a letter fell from beneath its folds.

Dear Kay,

I've been meaning to write to you for a long time. A very long time. It's been hard to write, and it seems the longer I've waited, the harder it gets.

I dreamt about you last night. In the dream we were back at Eleventh Street standing in the old brick yard. We were spitting cherry pits the way we used to, seeing who could spit them out the farthest.

The cherries were blood red, and you were only seven or eight, your hair a platinum color, the way it was the summer before Mom and Dad died.

It was strange. Dreams have a way of sneaking up on you, of sweeping you back to your past. In a matter of seconds you can travel back a lifetime. Imagine what it's like when you're old.

I hope you like the jacket. I made it extra big because I remember you used to like big, loose-fitting clothes. I don't know if you still do or even what size you wear, but I took a chance.

Happy birthday.

As you can see from my address I'm living in Nova Scotia now. Parts of it look like the pictures of Scotland that Dad took, remember?

I hope you're fine and well, and Jay and Georgia, too.

I miss you.

All my love,
Mattie

I didn't know what to think. I sat down hard at the kitchen table, as if I'd been struck dumb. She'd been gone four years this summer. I had not heard from her in three. No one had. And now this.

Kay. She was the only one who ever called me Kay. She called me Kay now and it made my heart dance and I didn't want it to dance. Four years.

And the jacket. It was meticulously made and the very thing I'd coveted since I was a little girl, and Mattie knew that. I got up and paced around the kitchen. Jay came in and pulled up a chair. I saw him take in the jacket on the table and the letter written on pale yellow stationery.

"She made the jacket," I told him.

He nodded. "Are you going to try it on?"

I slipped my arms into the cool silk sleeves and stood before the mirror in the living room. It fit me as if she'd taken my measurements. It was just loose enough to be comfortable without looking too big. I went back into the kitchen.

"What do you think?" My voice was hushed.

"It matches your hair," he said. He looked as if he might cry.

"What did she say?"

"Here, read it."

"No thanks."

"She's living in Nova Scotia. That's pretty much all she said." Not a word about Dean or how she really was or where she'd been for the past four years. "She said she hoped you were well," I told him. The color rose in his cheeks. He went to the fridge and stood there looking inside, as if he wanted something, and then he shut the door without taking anything and came and sat down.

"I don't understand it," I said.

"What?"

"Why she wrote. Why she made me the jacket. I don't understand any of it." He didn't answer me. I took off the jacket and put it back in the box.

"Are you going to tell Georgia?" Jay asked.

"I don't know."

"It'll make her crazy," he said. "It'll hurt her. Maybe that's what Mattie wants."

I shook my head. The air was suddenly heavy and dense with a pain so familiar, it made me want to cry.

"Isn't it just like Mattie," he said, picking up the box and holding it for a moment as if he were guessing it's weight. "It's all so calculated to win your heart."

"At least she wrote," I said in a flat voice.

"Yeah, that was big of her."

"Well, at least it's something."

"Is it?" he said. "You know what I think? It's a crumb. You could have been dead for all she knew, or me or Georgia. But it was nice of her to drop a line after all these years. Nice of her to keep in touch."

I thought of the tornado in *The Wizard of Oz*, of flat land and houses with storm cellars. There was no place here to hide from the storm. There never was.

We hardly spoke through dinner, and afterward I went up to my room and listened to music. Later I heard Jay's car pull out of the driveway. I thought of calling Celia up but decided not to. I took a long hot bath and washed my hair in the tub. I put on a pair of clean overalls and a striped T-shirt and an old pair of moccasins. And then I went up to the attic.

Right after Mattie left I used to spend a lot of time in her room, looking through her things, hoping to find a letter she'd meant to leave me. But there was no such note, for me or anyone else. There had been nothing to make her leaving any easier.

She had left her room surprisingly neat. Her drawings and sketchbook were all carefully put away in a large brown portfolio made of cardboard. Almost all her clothes were left in her drawers, for she had taken only what she could fit into a medium-size army knapsack. Her blue jean jacket still hung in the closet. She had sewn patches of red calico on the elbows and on the inside of the collar. Next to that was a dark blue cape she'd made out of gabardine, with a rose silk lining. Whenever she wore that cape people used to stop her and ask her where she'd bought it. There were a few cotton dresses hanging next to her winter coat and two or three skirts she'd made out of Laura Ashley material. At the back of her closet was a brown, antique trunk that had belonged to my grandmother, Sabrina. Mattie had had the foresight to lock the trunk, which I suspected contained her diaries and letters.

I walked around her room. I picked up objects and turned them over in my hand and put them down again: an empty box of Balkan Sobranies, a small frame containing an arrangement of pressed flowers under tinted glass. I had not been in here for two years. I had not wanted to be. I lay down on her bed and looked up at the ceiling.

One time, when Mattie was still going out with Will, I snuck up to her room and peered inside the door. It was almost dark outside, a winter twilight, and inside, the room was filled with a blue, shadowy light. Mattie and Will were lying on the bed together. She lay on top of him, fully clothed, her face pressed against his cheek. Stevie Wonder was playing softly on the record player. I stared at them for a moment, and then, without making a sound, I closed the door and went downstairs.

I'm not sure why I thought of that scene now, except that it was intimate and I had trespassed—and I was trespassing now.

I got up slowly and went to her closet. I dragged out the trunk, and then I sat down on the floor cross-legged and examined the lock. It was a small brass lock, and I tried to jiggle it but to no avail. Most likely she had taken the key with her. But then, I remembered there were usually two keys to a lock, and suddenly I knew where the second key must be.

Like a blind girl, my fingers searched through the bowl of blue-and-green beach glass. I found the small key on the bottom and closed my fist over it.

On the inside of the trunk's lid was my grandmother's name written in Russian with a blue fountain pen. She must have had this trunk when she was a child because the handwriting, although neat, was very childlike. There was a tray with compartments where Mattie had put away a few odds and ends. A small stack of embroidered handkerchiefs, a pink Spaulding ball, a baseball mitt my father had given her on her tenth birthday. I lifted out the tray and put it on the floor. The smell of lavender and must hit my nostrils and rose into the air like an invisible powder.

I almost cried out because the very first thing I saw was a photograph of my father I'd never seen before. It was glued onto a piece of red construction paper, which was the cover of a book Mattie had made. Under my father's photo were the words "My Father, by Mattie Sabrina Baker," written in a heavy, black Magic Marker. It was bound together like most school projects with three gold prongs that flattened out on the back page. On the first page was the title again and her name, and in the right-hand corner it read, Mrs. Fletcher, P.S. 41, Third Grade.

> My father is an English professor. He likes to read. He likes to teach. He has students and he gives them homework.

On the bottom of the page was a drawing done in crayons of a man in front of a red blackboard with one arm raised, as if he were pointing.

The second page read:

> My father was born in 1937, on Manhattan Island. My father can play baseball. My father can cook lamb stew.

Below there was a picture of a man running between two trees. On the third page it read:

My father married my mother. They had three children. I am the oldest. Jay is second. Kate is the baby.

I stared at the illustration. The family portrait. My parents were colorfully drawn, holding hands on one side of the page. An inch later came Mattie, about half their size, all in green except her hair, which was magenta. At the far corner of the page was a very small picture of me and Jay, all in yellow, our torsos stuck together like Siamese twins.

The last page of the book made me cry.

My father is very tall.
My father is very handsome.
My father knows God.

There was no picture here, but on the bottom the teacher had written, "A lovely job, Mattie!" in red pencil.

I closed the book and looked at the cover, and then I put it away. Mattie loved my father. I don't think there was anyone in the world she loved as much as him. And although I can never be sure, I think, perhaps, she was his favorite.

I laid the book aside and continued to look through the trunk. There was a pile of diaries and bunches of letters tied together with thin velvet ribbon. There was also a Capezio shoe box filled with snapshots I'd never seen. There were pictures of Will and Mattie taken in a photo booth. And some serious shots of Will standing with his back against a tree. There was a picture of me as a baby, sitting in Mattie's lap, and one of Jay, holding a neighbor's cat. There were lots of pictures of Mattie that Will must have taken and later, Dean. It was funny because she did not photograph well. Her features appeared too angular and sharp. There was no way you could tell from her photographs how really beautiful she was in life.

I closed the box of pictures, and then, after hesitating for a moment, I reached down and opened one of her diaries. There was only one line on the first page. It read:

For a long time I've been thinking about leaving.

I thought of my sister leaving on the back of a motorcycle. I thought of how much I loved her despite her strange silences and dark, moody ways. I thought of the good times we'd had. The summer night we'd played catch together under a soft rain. The time she taught me to waltz and we danced around her room in a circle until I was able to move almost as smoothly as she did. The times when my parents were still alive and she would baby-sit for me and Jay. She'd turn wild as soon as my parents were out the door, and being with her then was thrilling and hysterical, like the mounting excitement you feel on Christmas Eve.

There was the time she sewed all the sheets together to make a circus tent. And another when we played our own version of *Name That Tune.* Mattie stood at one end of the living room with her arms straight out to her sides, humming a song. Jay and I got so good, all we needed were the first two notes and we'd be tearing across the room tagging her hands yelling, "This Land is Your Land," or "Michael Row the Boat Ashore" at the top of our lungs. I thought of how all my life I'd looked up to my sister and been afraid of her, never knowing if she'd be kind or fun or distant or cold. Never really knowing from one minute to the next what she was going to do or where she was going to go.

I put everything away and went downstairs. Georgia came home at midnight, and I pretended to be asleep. Outside my window, the light from the moon was bone-white, eerie. I lay awake for hours.

CHAPTER TEN

When I jumped off the rock at Alexander Falls, I pretended I was jumping off a building. I half expected my life to flash before me the way they say it does right before you die. But nothing like that happened, and instead I was a cartoon character trying to stop herself in midair, legs running as if on land, arms flailing about. When I hit the water, it was cold enough to stop my heart. I thought I might never surface. Toes pointed, I sank as fast as a rocket, but then I touched bottom and up I went, practically flying out of the water.

"You know, you're crazy," Celia said, throwing me a towel. "You're much too brave for me."

"It's nothing," I said, my ears ringing with cold. I dragged myself onto the bank. "The real trick is breathing underwater."

78

"Why would you do such a thing?" Aunt Georgia asked me that night. "What's gotten into you?" I sat in the kitchen, shivering in my bathrobe as she poured me a cup of tea. Celia gave me a sympathetic glance and patted my shoulder. "I'm sorry, Kate, but I have to go. I hope you don't get sick."

"Honestly, Kate," Georgia scolded. "It's so unlike you to do something so dangerous."

I caught Jay staring at me and I looked away. The rock at the falls was thirty feet high, and it was illegal to jump off it, although people still did. Five years ago, a seventeen-year-old boy was killed because he hadn't jumped out far enough, and instead of hitting the water, he'd hit the rocks.

Jay drove Celia home, and I sat in the kitchen with Georgia and drank another cup of tea. But I couldn't stop shaking, and Georgia made me get into bed. She brought me another quilt from the linen closet.

"I'm very angry with you," she said, laying the quilt over me.

"I know you are."

"Well, what's going on here?"

"Nothing."

"Nothing! You just felt like jumping off a cliff, that's it?"

"It was a rock, Georgia, not a cliff."

"Promise me you won't do anything like this again."

"I promise."

"You know, you don't look well," she said. She felt my forehead and left the room for a minute, coming back with a thermometer. I had a slight fever, and Georgia made me take some aspirin and drink a large glass of juice.

"Try to get some rest," she said gruffly. "And no more acrobatics. It does something to my heart." She bent down and kissed my cheek, and then she left the room, closing the door behind her.

As soon as she left, I started to cry. Hearing from Mattie had made me miss her all over again. It was as if I were suddenly twelve years old and she had just run away.

It was hard to fall asleep, and when I did, I dreamed about my parents. It was the same dream I used to have right after they died. In the dream I was swimming underwater with my mother and father. The ocean was phosphorescent green, and my mother's long hair sparkled like gold down her back.

"You're here," I said. "You've come back."

"Everything's all right now," she said, taking my hand. We swam together, and I saw that everything I knew was underwater—my school, my house, the park, everything. My father turned his head and smiled at me, and I waved back.

"Will it always be like this?" I asked my mother.

"Always," she said, and I was happy. The water shimmered blue and then green, a kaleidoscope of light. We swam on and on, like a school of fish, and then I woke up.

"Feeling better?" Georgia asked me on Sunday night. I had spent the weekend at home, wandering aimlessly around the house in my pajamas.

"I'm fine now," I told her.

"That's good," she said. We sat on her bed and ate pizza together. The *Berkshire Eagle* and the Sunday *New York Times* were strewn around her room.

I looked at the Travel section of the *Times.* There was an article about Wales. "I'd like to go to Wales," I said.

"Is there anyplace you *don't* want to visit, Katie?" she said, laughing.

"Hmm, I have to think about that."

Georgia was going through a shoe box in which she kept letters and documents. "What are you looking for?" I asked.

"A receipt."

"For what?"

"A patchwork quilt I bought years ago. I found it in the closet yesterday. It's a good one, worth a lot of money. I want to find out when it was made. The year was written on the receipt."

"Are you going to sell it?"

"Maybe. Oh, look at this," she said. She'd taken a blue envelope from the box. It was addressed to Georgia in my mother's small, neat script. I knew my mother's handwriting from the books she'd inscribed to me on Christmases and birthdays. On the back of the envelope she'd drawn a picture in green and purple ink of an African violet.

Dearest Georgia,

Thanks so much for the lovely bunting. It will come in handy, I'm sure. Yesterday we brought Mattie home from the hospital. She is so beautiful and so alert and only seven days old! John is over the moon, as you can imagine.

It's terrible that you have the flu. You must get over it fast and come and see us as soon as possible. We miss you very much and cannot wait to introduce you to your niece.

Hurry and get well.

All my love and kisses,
Nell

Georgia handed me the letter. "Perhaps," she said softly, "you might like to keep this?"

"Thank you." I put my arms around my aunt and kissed her cheek. The letter had upset her. It had made her think of Mattie and of her leaving. I wanted to tell her that I knew where my sister was, but I was too scared. That would be like reopening Pandora's box, and I was afraid of the consequences.

Before going to bed I put the letter on my dresser next to a picture of my mother. I stared at my mother's photograph while I brushed my hair. For the first time I wondered what my mother would think of

Mattie living all the way in Nova Scotia. I took out my atlas and looked at Canada.

I didn't know very much about Nova Scotia. On the map it looked small and vulnerable, sticking out into the Atlantic Ocean. I pictured it as being very cold and white in the winter, and damp with the smell of seawater. I thought of my sister over a thousand miles away, and I knew the time had come for me to see her.

CHAPTER ELEVEN

"I have a person-to-person call for Mattie Hartwell," said the operator. There was a pause, an almost imperceptible hesitation, and then, "This is she."

"Go ahead," said the operator.

"Hi . . . it's me."

"Hello, Kate." My heart pounded, and I had to stop myself from yelling, "*You're alive, you're really there!*"

"How are you? How are you, Mattie?"

"I'm all right," she said softly. "What about you?"

"I'm fine. I'm good, I guess. I don't know." It was hard to talk. I was not quite twelve when I'd last heard her voice. I wondered what it was like for people who hadn't spoken to each other in twenty or fifty years. I wondered if it was anything like this. Outside, the traffic moved down a one-way street. I stood in the phone booth with dollars-worth of change lined up on the shelf.

"I got the jacket," I told her.

"I know." Of course she knew. How else would I have known where to reach her? "Does it fit?"

"Yes, perfectly."

"I'm glad. I wasn't sure if it would."

"No, it does. It really does. It's beautiful."

"The color reminded me of you," she said. "Wheat color."

We both fell silent. I tried to imagine where she was standing or sitting and what her house was like.

"How are Jay and Georgia?" she asked.

"They're fine. What's . . . what's it like in Nova Scotia?"

"Oh, it's very beautiful and kind of strange. It's nothing like the States. . . . It's hard to explain."

"Are you happy?" I asked. "Are you happy, Mattie?"

"I don't know," she said. "Sometimes." There was another pause while we both waited for the other to speak.

"I'd like to come see you."

"You mean, come to Canada?"

"Yes." Outside, the sun was so bright it hurt my eyes and I found myself squinting. "I need to see you, Mattie." There was a long silence and we both listened to it.

"Of course you can come, Kate," she said finally. "I'd like that."

When I hung up the phone, I burst into tears. I don't know what I would have done if she had said no. I felt as if my life were standing still and the only way it could move forward was to see Mattie.

"Absolutely not!" Georgia said.

"Why? Why not?"

"I won't have you running around Canada."

"I won't be running around anyplace. I'll be going to see Mattie."

"Why can't she come here?"

"I don't know. I asked if I could visit *her*, Georgia. She didn't say anything about coming here."

"Four years and this is the best she can do?" Georgia's face had gone white when I'd told her about Mattie.

"Look, Georgia, I just want to see her. I don't see why I can't do that."

"It's not right," she said. "Why hasn't she written to *me*?"

"I don't know," I said.

Mattie had never been as close to Georgia as Jay or I. But after our parents died she moved away from everyone. We'd be sitting at the dinner table and she'd recede into herself, her face stiff and tight, like a person trying to hide a great physical pain.

"She would never let me comfort her. She would never let me love her the way you and Jay did."

"She never let *anyone* comfort her, except Dad," I said. "She was always private."

I thought of one Halloween when Mattie, in white-face and dressed in a Japanese robe, had gone as a Kabuki actor. There was something so like Mattie in that white mask, all the emotion under layers of a delicate powder.

"Georgia, let me go see her. I'll only stay for a week. Just let me see her."

The room was hot and airless, and Georgia was in tears.

"You're not going, Kate. That's all there is to it."

"You can't stop me from seeing my sister."

"She can come here."

"No! Don't you see, I don't think she'll come."

"Well, I'm not going to spend the rest of my life catering to her. She has to make some goddamn effort!"

"I see the news of the century has been revealed at last," said Jay, coming into the kitchen with a bag of groceries. I turned my back on him and faced my aunt. "Am I the *only* one who still cares about Mattie?"

"I will not discuss this anymore!"

"But—"

"You're not going!" Georgia screamed at me. She ran from the room and up the stairs.

"That's nice," said Jay. "That was thoughtful of you."

"Shut up."

"Happy now?"

"What is *wrong* with you? You're making it all my fault. I want to see my sister. Is that a crime in this house?"

"You think you're some kind of messenger now? The chosen one who gets to rescue the lost sister?"

"I just want to see her. You care about her, too, Jay."

"Do I? I don't think so. You see, unlike you, I gave up a long time ago. It used to kill me that she'd ignore me all the time, that she preferred you. But there's only so much damage you can let a person do. She's selfish, Kate."

"She's our sister!"

"You're missing the point. Mattie doesn't love anyone but herself. How can she? She's incapable. But you refuse to see that."

"No, I don't. I know she has faults."

"Has faults? Everyone has faults! It's *beyond* that with her. She thinks God created the whole world for her."

"I still love her!" I yelled. "You can't make me stop loving her!"

He shook his head sadly. "Sometimes I think if she was dead, this would still be happening. That somehow, even as a corpse, she'd still have the power to tear us all apart."

I turned and left the house. I half walked and half

ran down the road. It was just starting to get dark by the time I reached Celia's. There were no lights on in the house, and the car was gone. I sat down on her front step and waited. Humphrey, the dog from across the road, came trotting over to me. He was a sweet, funny-looking mutt with a tawny coat.

"Hi, Humphrey," I said. He wagged his tail and plopped down on my feet. "How are you doing, boy? How are you doing?" His tail began thumping like mad, and I started to cry. "You're a good boy," I told him. "Good dog." I sat outside petting Humphrey until it grew dark, and then he got up and crossed the road, heading for home. A car pulled up the driveway. I wiped my eyes and rose to my feet. It was Jay.

"Come on, Kate," he said. I sat back down and turned my head away from him. He came and sat beside me.

"Nobody understands," I said after a while. He shrugged.

"Maybe not."

"She's being crazy, not letting me go."

"Try to understand how she feels."

"Well, I don't."

"Don't you? Why can't Mattie come here, anyway? She's a big girl." His voice was bitter.

"She wouldn't come. I just know it."

"Well, I think you're nuts to go. What has she ever done for you? What has she ever done for anyone?"

It was suddenly chilly, and I found myself shivering.

"I'm going to see her," I said quietly. "I have to go." He didn't answer. "I'm not trying to hurt anyone."

"I know."

"I'm going for *me*. . . . I . . ."

"Look, you don't have to explain it to me."

"But I don't want you to be mad at me, Jay."

"Oh, I'll get over it," he said. "But I can't help feeling the way I do about Mattie. I hate her for leaving us, for making us feel like we were dirt, like we were something she had to get away from."

"Part of me hates her, too," I said. "For putting me in the middle all the time, for making everything so difficult. But it's been so long since I've seen her— Don't you see, Jay, I don't know *who* she is anymore."

"Well, maybe that's the difference between us," he said softly. "Because I don't care who she is. I guess I just don't care anymore."

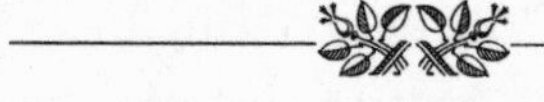

CHAPTER TWELVE

Dear Georgia,

I've gone to see Mattie. Please don't be angry with me. I have enough money and I've made all the arrangements, so don't worry. I'll call you as soon as I get there.

I love you, Georgia, and I never want to hurt you, but this is something I must do.

Kate

I waited until Georgia went to work, and then I put the letter on her bureau. From the back of my closet I pulled out an old green knapsack, the same one my mother used when she was seventeen and traveling through Europe with my father.

I packed lightly—jeans, a few shirts, a warm sweater, a poncho. I also packed the letter my mother had written to Georgia. I thought Mattie would want

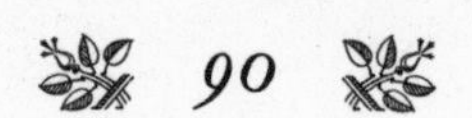

it. At the last minute I took a diary Celia's mother had given to me one Christmas. I'd never used it. I decided to travel in my blue jean overalls because they were soft and comfortable and because of all the pockets.

I loved pockets—they made me feel safe and compact. I've never liked carrying a bag. I liked to have everything on me, so to speak—my comb, money. I liked to be self-contained.

I glanced around my room to see if I'd forgotten anything. I looked at the photos on my walls, at the map over my bed. For years I'd longed to have a passport with stamps from every country. I had longed to speak at least five languages, all fluently and brilliantly. I had longed for adventure.

Now I was going to Canada, to a place I'd never been. I tried not to think of how hurt and angry Georgia would be. For the first time in my life I was doing something on my own. And the terror and excitement I felt was as powerful as anything I'd ever known.

I heard Celia honking outside, and I grabbed my pack and the jacket Mattie had made me and raced downstairs. Celia had borrowed her mother's car for the day.

"Where to first?" she asked.

"The bank."

"Okay."

"What's the matter?" I asked. She looked uneasy.

"Nothing . . . I . . . Are you sure about all this?"

"I'm sure."

"All right," she said, staring at me with her large hazel eyes. We drove to the bank in silence.

I took two hundred dollars out of my savings, leaving one dollar so they wouldn't close my account. The cheapest way to travel to Nova Scotia was to take the ferry from Bar Harbor, Maine. My plan was to take the bus to Boston, and from there I'd get a bus to Maine. I had calculated that the trip would cost about a hundred and fifty dollars. I was afraid Charlotte, the bank teller, would ask what I needed so much money for. But luckily Charlotte wasn't there, and a new person, a skittish young man I'd never seen before, took care of me. The whole time I was in the bank, I was terrified I'd run into someone I knew and that somehow that person would know just by looking at me what I had planned.

When we got back to the car, I practically jumped inside. "Let's get out of here," I said.

"We're going, we're going," said Celia. The bus left from Lee, and as we drove there, I took out my wallet and counted my money again.

"What's that?" Celia said, nodding at my lap.

"My birth certificate."

"You don't need a passport to get into Canada?"

"No, a birth certificate is fine."

"Well, I wouldn't keep it in your wallet if I were you. You should always carry your money and identification separately."

"Oh." I put my wallet in my side pocket. I took out

my diary and stuck the birth certificate in its center.

"Now, what am I going to say to Georgia?" Celia asked. "I know she'll call me."

"Tell her the truth." I didn't want Celia to have to lie. "Tell her that you put me on the bus to Boston."

"She'll be furious with me."

"No, she won't. I'm the one she'll be furious with."

"What about Jay? He seems pretty upset lately."

"He knows I'm going, but he doesn't know when." She gave me a funny look. "He didn't *want* to know, Ceil."

"Well, I don't like this whole thing," she said. I was afraid for a moment she might turn the car around, but she didn't.

When we got to Lee, I bought my ticket in the drugstore along with a couple of candy bars, and then I went outside to wait with Celia.

"Do you have everything?" she asked.

"I think so." She bit her fingernail. "I have to go, Ceil."

"I guess if you have to, you have to," she said. She glanced around nervously. She was wearing an old red-and-white checked shirt of Jay's.

"You look nice in that shirt," I told her.

"Kate . . ."

"It's going to be okay," I said. "Really." She nodded at me, unconvinced.

"I just don't think you should go like this."

"It's the only way I can go."

"Well, it seems crazy."

"Look there's my bus," I said with relief. We both watched as the bus driver got out and opened up a side panel and helped people put their luggage inside. He came around to the door and started taking tickets.

"Be careful," she whispered.

"I will." We hugged. "I love you, Ceil."

"I love you too, Kate. Don't forget to send me a postcard!" she yelled as I started up the steps.

"I won't."

"Good-bye."

"Good-bye!"

There were quite a few people already on the bus, but I found a seat in the middle by a window. I knocked on the glass and waved to Celia. She waved back, a tentative, nervous wave. She stood there watching until the bus left, her arms folded across her chest in a motherly stance that was worried and self-protective at the same time.

I settled back in my seat. I'd forgotten to bring a book, but then I was too keyed-up to read. It would take three hours to get to Boston, and from there I'd have a four-hour wait before boarding a bus to Maine.

It was my day off from work, and had it been a normal day, I'd have gone swimming with Celia in the Green River, or maybe we'd have gone to an afternoon movie. But here I was on a bus on my way to visit Mattie. And I had to keep telling myself what it was that I was doing, over and over like a chant of faith.

95

I took out my diary and stared at the blank pages. I didn't know how Mattie had written so much, how she knew what to write. Once, in a candid moment, I'd asked her why she wrote and she said, "Because then it makes everything real."

I didn't like the idea of writing on the first page, so I skipped a few pages and wrote, "I'm on my way to see Mattie." I didn't know what else to say, so I closed the book. I took out my wallet and looked at my ticket, and then I counted my money again.

In the side compartment of my wallet I kept some photographs. One was of me and Jay and Celia taken in a photo booth, all squished together with our tongues out at the camera. There was a photo of my parents and an old one of Mattie with her hands on her hips and her hair in two braids like Pippi Longstocking. The last one was of Georgia standing in the garden among her new roses with a big smile on her face.

"Come look at my roses, Katie," she'd said to me in June when they had first bloomed, the palest of pink roses. She was wearing her old straw hat with a white band around its brim.

"Oh, they smell so good," I said, bending over the soft, fragrant petals. I loved flowers, not just roses but tiger lilies and forget-me-nots, violets. All kinds.

"I think I'm flower-crazy, Georgia," I'd told her. "Just like you."

"Not a bad way to be, Cookie," she'd said, slipping her arm around me.

I put the pictures away. Right now Georgia was working in the store, wrapping gifts in purple tissue paper, sipping coffee out of her large white mug. I hoped she would forgive me for leaving. I knew she did not expect me to go.

For as long as I could remember Mattie had been the wild one, while I was the good girl. And from the time she ran away I'd felt I had to stay home and protect what was left of my family.

I sat up straight and shook my head. I did not want to think about Georgia or Mattie or anyone else. I had hardly slept these past few nights, and I was exhausted. I closed my eyes and tried to sleep. The bus was air-conditioned, and it was freezing. I draped my jacket over my head. The chamois and the silk had a nice new smell.

When at last I fell asleep, my dreams were filled with a weird, opaque light. They were full of ghostly images and of familiar people who floated and wavered and were always just out of reach.

CHAPTER THIRTEEN

The Boston bus station was crowded with people moving around in that semipanicked way people have when they're catching buses or trains. I was on the way to the ladies' room when I felt someone bump against my back. I turned around.

"Excuse me," a young woman said. She looked me straight in the eyes and smiled apologetically. She was cool in a summer dress and had a lacy shawl draped over one arm. I smiled back.

"That's all right," I said.

In the ladies' room there was a girl my age with stringy hair giving a baby a bath in one of the sinks. When I came out of the toilet, she was drying the baby with paper towels.

"Got the time?" she asked. She wore powder-blue shorts and a bright yellow halter top.

"It's six-fifteen," I said.

"Thanks."

I had almost four hours before my bus left for Maine, and I didn't want to spend them in the bus station. I sat down on a bench and took out my map of Boston. Maps were such wonderful things. You could look at a map and know just where you were.

"Where are you going?" a voice said. I turned and saw a boy of eighteen or so sitting next to me. He had jet-black hair and a tanned face. His eyes were startling. They reminded me of pictures I'd once seen of the Caribbean—turquoise.

"I'm on my way to Maine. But I have hours before my next bus and I don't want to wait here."

"Can't see why not," he said, and then he laughed. "Bus stations are notoriously depressing, aren't they?"

"And seedy," I said. He smiled at me and was about to speak when a small boy came running by us and tripped, falling hard on his stomach. The young man jumped to his feet and helped him up.

"You okay?" he asked gently. The boy wailed. "Hey, you're all right it's just a fall, a bad fall." The boy stopped crying and stared at the young man. A distraught little girl came running over.

"Stanley, there you are!" She swept the boy up in her skinny arms and hurried away with him.

"Poor little Stanley," said the young man. I smiled.

"My name is Max," he said, extending his hand.

"Kate." We shook hands, and he turned my hand over in his own.

"Do you play piano?" he asked.

"No, why?"

"You have piano-player hands."

"I play chopsticks."

"That must be it," he said, and I laughed.

"Where are you going?" I asked.

"New Hampshire. I'm picking up my sister here, and we're driving up together."

"My brother went camping in the White Mountains last summer," I said.

"It's a great state," he said. "My family has a cabin near Hanover. It belonged to my grandmother. No one uses it anymore, except me and Lindsey. That's my sister." He glanced at the clock on the far wall. "Her bus is late. She's going to be in a terrible mood when she gets here."

"Where's she coming from?"

"North Carolina. Our father lives there."

"Are you from North Carolina?" I asked. He didn't have a Southern accent.

"I lived there until I was ten, and then my mother remarried and we moved to Plymouth. What about you? Where are you from?"

"I was born in New York, but I live in the Berkshires."

"Oh, really, what part?"

"West Stockbridge."

"No kidding. I have a good friend who lives in Great Barrington. She works at the movie theater there."

"Oh, sure. Who's your friend?"

"Sara Brooks."

"I *know* Sara!" She was two years older than Jay, and she'd worked in Georgia's store a few summers ago. She was a tall, soft-spoken girl with hair down to her waist. Whenever business was slow at Georgia's, she'd sit on a stool behind the counter and read mystery novels. "She's nice," I told Max.

"Yes, she is. My mother is an old friend of her mother's. When we were little, our families used to spend Thanksgiving together."

He took a Granny Smith from his pocket. "Would you like an apple? I have another one."

"No thanks."

He wiped the apple on his shirt. "It's wild, our both knowing Sara, isn't it?"

"Yes, it is."

He took a bite of the apple, and the juice sprayed right in my face. "Oh, I'm sorry!" he said. I wiped my face with the back of my hand. He looked frantically in his pocket for a tissue; but I told him it was all right.

"This must be some crazy trick apple," he said, and I laughed. He looked at me closely, as if he were taking me in.

"Do you go to school?" I asked when he'd composed himself.

"Just graduated. High school, that is. Boy, I never thought I'd see the day. I'm a terrible student. The opposite of my sister. Anyway, the last thing I wanted was to go to college. And just between us, I don't think there's a place on earth that would have me. So I've saved up some money, and I'm going to New Orleans in September."

"What's in New Orleans?"

"Music. Dixieland, jazz. I can't wait." He told me he had started playing the guitar a few years ago and that he wanted to be a musician.

"What about you? Do you go to college?" he asked.

I told him I had one more year of high school and I wanted to take a year off to travel when I graduated.

"Where do you want to go?"

"Oh, everywhere. . . ."

As we were talking I noticed a vending machine nearby. "I'm going to get a soda," I told him. "Do you want one?"

"No thanks."

It was fifty cents for a Coke. I put my hand in my pocket and my heart jumped. My wallet was gone.

"Oh, no." I turned the pocket inside out and felt along the lining of the jacket to see if it could have dropped through a hole. I felt all the pockets in my overalls.

"What's the matter?" Max asked.

"I can't find my wallet." I knelt on the floor and ripped through my entire knapsack.

"It's gone," I told him. I could feel the tears coming. All my money was gone and my ticket, too. And the photographs. "This is terrible," I said. Three hours from home and I was unable to take care of myself.

"When did you see it last?" Max said.

"On the bus right before I got off. I put it in this pocket."

"It must have fallen out."

"Maybe, but I don't think so. It's a pretty deep pocket."

"Well, let's go look for it. We'll retrace your steps."

We went outside the station and looked on the ground and then came back in the way I had before.

"Even if I did drop it somewhere, someone probably picked it up and kept it. I had almost one hundred and fifty dollars in it. My whole savings." The palms of my hands were starting to sweat.

"Where did you go from here?" he asked.

"I . . . I went over there and . . ."

"What?"

"Nothing. A lady bumped into me, but . . ."

"But what?"

"I don't think she . . . she was too well dressed to . . ."

"To pick your pocket? Are you kidding? It's a whole racket with people. They dress up so you won't suspect them. But just to make sure we should still check all the places you went."

I kept praying I'd see my wallet. I had this crazy hope that it would turn up, that I'd see a glimpse of red somewhere, and that would be it.

I went back into the ladies' room and looked in the stall I'd used—nothing. I followed my steps to the bench where I'd met Max.

"I've checked with the lost and found," he said. "They don't have it."

"You were right," I said. "She must have taken it."

"Excuse me," she'd said, looking straight at me. Of course she'd taken it. Why else would she have been so bold as to look me in the eye? Anyone else would have averted their eyes. People get embarrassed when they're clumsy.

"She took it all right," I told him. "Oh, God, I don't know what to do."

"Can't you call home?" I shook my head. Everything was ruined now. I sat down on top of my knapsack with my face in my hands.

"I'm so stupid," I said.

"It's not your fault. It could happen to anyone." I shook my head. How was I going to get to Mattie's now? I couldn't very well call home and say, "Oh, by the way, could you send me enough money to get to Nova Scotia? You see, I've had my wallet stolen . . ." It was no use. I had done a terrible thing by leaving, and now I was being punished. I was incompetent and stupid. If I couldn't even get to Boston in one piece, how would I ever get to Canada?

"What am I going to do?"

"I could lend you some money. How much was the ticket?" I told him it was fifty altogether, thirty-eight to get to Maine. He said he was sorry, but he didn't have that much on him.

"And then I'll need another fifteen for the ferry," I said.

"*Where* are you going?" he said.

"To Nova Scotia."

"Oh." He looked at me closely. "Are you running away, Kate?"

"No, I'm going to see my sister."

"You don't have to tell me," he said, suddenly uncomfortable. "It's none of my business."

"I don't mind telling you, Max." It was a relief to talk to someone. I told him about Mattie running away. "Nobody's seen her in years, and, well, nobody knows I'm going to see her except Celia. She's my best friend. And my brother Jay knows, but he doesn't know when. You see, he didn't think I should go. And my Aunt Georgia, we live with her, she didn't want me to go at all. She said Mattie should come to us. But I knew Mattie wouldn't come, so I had to go on my own." I said this all in a great rush, because I was afraid that if I didn't say it fast, I would start to cry. Max stared at me, but he didn't say anything.

"I think I'll look through my knapsack again," I

said, even though I knew it was useless. I opened my knapsack and began to take everything out. I felt a light hand on my shoulder.

"Listen, I'm sorry, but I have to go meet my sister. Her bus is due any minute."

"That's okay, I understand. Well, good-bye." I shook his hand. He was nice and kind, and when he left, I'd be all alone. "Thanks for helping me look for my wallet."

"Are you going to be okay? What are you going to do?"

"I'll call my friend Celia. And if she's not there, then I guess I'll call home and someone will pick me up." It was a dismal thought.

"Don't you need some money to call?"

"No thanks. I've got some change."

"Well, good luck," he said. He seemed reluctant to leave, and I knew he felt sorry for me. "I hope everything works out okay."

"Good-bye, Max." I watched him walk away.

I shook out my clothes one more time and turned my knapsack inside out. The great feeling of excitement I'd had all day had disappeared, and I was beginning to feel a kind of numbing panic take over. For a moment I thought of calling Andy, but I knew there wasn't much he could do for me. I knew I had to call home, and postponing it any longer was silly.

I tried Celia first, but there was no answer.

"Where are you, Ceil?" I whispered. I hung up, and

then I picked up the receiver again but didn't dial.

"Are you using the phone?" a woman said.

"What?"

"Are you making a call?" She was impatient.

"Yes, yes, I am." I turned my back on her and called home. My stomach had tightened into a giant knot at the mere thought of speaking to Georgia. I had no idea what to say to her. The phone rang and rang, and at last I hung up. I forced myself to try the shop, but there was no one there, either. I must have just missed her.

The woman waiting for the phone had lit a cigarette.

"Are you done yet?" she asked.

"Yes," I told her. "Yes, I'm done."

I walked back to the bench where I'd met Max. I didn't know what to do, so I took out my address book and read through all the names and addresses I'd collected over the years. But the only people in the book I could call were Celia and Jay. Will was in there, but I no longer felt close to Will. I still loved him. I'd probably always love him, but it wasn't the same as before. I didn't trust him anymore.

The thought of Will made me even more depressed, and I started to cry.

"Hey, what's the matter, girlie?" a man said. He was creepy-looking, with watery blue eyes. I jumped up and moved away. How could this whole thing happen? I asked myself. The man was still staring at me. I started to go outside.

"Kate, Kate!" someone called. I wondered who knew me in this crowd of strangers, and then I realized it was Max.

"Max!"

"There you are! Next to him was a slender, dark-haired girl.

"Kate, this is my sister, Lindsey."

"Hello," she said. She was wearing white jeans and a yellow T-shirt with a map of San Francisco on it. Her narrow face was partially hidden by a pair of large black sunglasses. She reminded me of someone, but I could not think of who it was.

"I told Lindsey about your wallet being stolen."

"It happened to me at a concert once," she said. "It's a horrible feeling."

"Did you reach home?" Max said.

"No one was there. I'll have to try later." I must have looked distraught because Max said they'd wait with me.

"Oh, no, I don't know how long it will be."

"Can we give you a ride somewhere?" Lindsey asked. She seemed anxious to go.

"Yes, maybe you should come with us," Max said. "We're not exactly going in your direction. You want to go northeast and we're going northwest, but it's something."

"But . . ."

"And I can lend you money when we get to the cabin. I have cash up there, emergency money."

"I'd lend you some money, but I'm flat broke," Lindsey said. I thanked her anyway. "Is there a bus station near your cabin?" I asked.

"There's one in Vermont, in White River Junction. That's not far from us at all. I know they have buses that go to Portland, and you could probably change there and get a bus to take you the rest of the way."

"Are you sure you don't mind?"

"Not at all."

I thought about my choices. I could either wait for Jay or Georgia to come pick me up, or I could continue on my way with Max and Lindsey.

"Are you *sure* it's all right?" I asked again.

"Of course."

"I promise to pay you back as soon as I can."

"Oh, I know you will," Max said. "I can tell you're the honest type."

CHAPTER FOURTEEN

We picked up Highway 93 and headed toward New Hampshire. I sat up front with Max, and Lindsey lay in the back reading *People* magazine.

Max's car was a 1962 British-racing-green Volvo. It had an old-fashioned shape with a sloped front and a metal grille.

"This is such a great car," I said.

"She's a beaut, isn't she? I wish I had more money to put into her. She needs work all the time. Still, I'm never going to sell her. When she gets too old to run, I'll keep her on my front lawn."

"Like a large art piece," I said.

"Right."

"Max, can you turn down the radio a little?" Lindsey asked.

"She doesn't like jazz," he said. "What about you?"

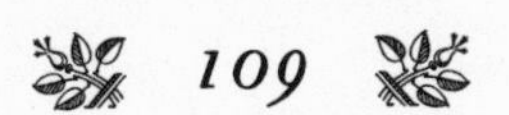

"I like jazz," Lindsey said, "but I have to be in the mood for it. I'm just not in the mood for it right now."

Max turned down the volume.

"I love Billie Holiday and Ella Fitzgerald," I told him.

"They're great," he said. He told me his favorite musicians were Charlie Christian and Django Rhinhart.

"Max, are you going to be stopping soon?" Lindsey asked.

"Why?"

"I want to try Teddy."

"Pretty soon," he said. "We need some gas."

We stopped for gas a little while later, and Lindsey made a phone call. The phone booth was outside, and she had her back to us. Max and I stayed in the car and shared a candy bar.

"This might be a long one," he said, nodding at his sister.

"Who's Teddy?"

"Her boyfriend. An Amherst man. Lindsey goes to Smith. They're both brilliant. Straight-*A* types, full scholarships, the works."

"Do you like him?"

"I do, actually. He's one of those people who you like right away but you're not sure why. He's comfortable to be around."

Like Will, I thought.

"He never tried to impress me. Lindsey's old boyfriend, Scott, used to hang around my room talking about football. I don't even like football. He was trying so hard to be my *pal*, you know. And I never understood why he thought we had to be friends, just because he was going out with my sister."

I remembered an afternoon with Dean. He had come to see Mattie, but she wasn't back from school yet. He asked Jay if he wanted to ride on his motorcycle.

"No thanks," Jay had said, going inside and slamming the door behind him, leaving Dean stunned.

"What about you, Kate?" Dean asked. I could tell he was trying to save face by asking me.

"Okay." I thought if I went, I'd know what it felt like to be Mattie. But then Georgia came out and said, "Absolutely not," and how there was no way that she'd let me on the back of any motorcycle. I started to protest, but then Mattie came home and Dean forgot all about me.

"You can usually tell," Max said to me, "when someone is being sincere."

"Instinct," I said.

"Yes, instinct."

We saw Lindsey turn around and wave to us. "Do you have any change?" she yelled. "I've run out."

Max got out of the car. I watched him dig deep into his jeans pocket and hand her some coins. She held the receiver against her stomach and whispered something to him.

"Take your time," I heard him say. "Hey, want a soda?" he called out to me.

"Sure."

I got out of the car and stretched my legs.

"All they had was Orange Crush," he said, handing me a bottle.

"Thanks. I like almost anything with orange in it."

"Do you? I bet you love Creamsicles."

"Yes. What about you?"

"I'm a chocolate freak. Fudgesicles, chocolate éclairs, chocolate-chip ice cream on a stick."

"Snickers, Heath bars," I said.

"Chunkies, Three Musketeers, Peppermint Patties." We both started to laugh. I looked up at him. He was a few inches taller than me and quite thin. His face was angular with high cheekbones and a long, straight nose. He was wearing a khaki shirt that looked like an army shirt. His hair was blue-black in the fading sunlight.

"I can't believe my wallet was stolen," I said. "And you know what's terrible?"

"What?"

"I *smiled* at the woman who stole it. She bumped into me and I *smiled* at her." I shook my head.

"Hey, what are you two standing around for?" Lindsey said. She'd taken off her sunglasses, and I saw that she had the same blue eyes as Max. Her hair was cut short, just below her earlobes, and I realized who she reminded me of. Audrey Hepburn.

"How's Teddy?" Max asked.

"He's fine," she said, smiling.

"Ready to go?" he said.

"Ready."

We drove straight to New Hampshire without stopping. I lay in the backseat with my eyes closed listening to the jazz station. Duke Ellington's "The Queen's Suite." And then Nat King Cole singing "Sweet Lorraine" and "It's Only a Paper Moon." It was oddly comforting riding in the car with Max and Lindsey. Everything had gone haywire, but I wasn't stranded and I wasn't alone. I felt lucky to have met Max.

"You okay back there?" he asked.

"Fine."

"Music too loud?"

"No."

After a while I dozed off. I didn't want to sleep, but the motion of the car made me sleepy. When I woke up, the sky was black, and I could hear the hum of traffic and the rush of the wind through the windows. I lay very still. Max and Lindsey were talking, and I knew from their conversation that they believed I was sleeping.

"So, what was it like seeing Dad?" Max asked.

"It was okay."

"How is he?"

"The same. What's-her-name was there every second."

"You know her name, Lindsey."

"I can't believe he's going to marry her."

"She's all right. In a way she's nicer than he is. At least *she* listens."

"When did you get so crazy about her?"

"I'm not crazy about her. I just think she's okay."

"Well, I don't. Have you ever had a conversation with her?"

"Sure. The last time I saw Dad, there was an outdoor concert in Chapel Hill. Dad didn't want to go, so I went with Delia."

"What did you talk about?"

"We talked about music and, I don't know, ice cream."

"Ice cream?"

"Yeah, she makes it from scratch."

"Sounds fascinating."

"You're too hard on her, Lindsey."

"She's my age! How can he marry someone my age?"

"He loves her."

"Oh, *please*. The whole thing is pathetic. They don't even *know* anyone to invite to the wedding. She doesn't have any girlfriends, and he's lost touch with his old friends."

"Who *are* they inviting?"

"You, me. Delia's grandmother, who lives in a

nursing home. Tom Brower, the guy from Dad's office. And that's it. She had to pay extra for the invitations because the printer said fifty was the minimum."

"I feel sorry for her."

"Why? I don't. You know, while I was there she was making her wedding dress. She tried it on for me and asked what kind of veil I thought she should buy."

"What did you say?"

"I said I thought veils were tacky."

"Lindsey!"

"And then she looked as if she were going to cry, so I said not *all* veils. I ended up sitting on the bed with her helping her choose a veil from *Brides* magazine."

All the time Lindsey was talking, an image of Delia was developing before my eyes like a Polaroid picture. I saw her as sweet and plain-looking with pale red hair, a little on the skinny side.

"The whole thing is a fiasco," Lindsey said. "And you know what the hilarious part is?"

"What?" He sounded depressed.

"She wants me to be her maid of honor."

"I'm starting to get a headache," Max said.

The car was quiet for a minute. I heard a rustling sound and then a match being lit.

"Open your window if you're going to smoke," Max said.

"I don't know why I went to see Dad in the first place," she said. "It's not as if he makes an effort to see me. And then, when I do see him, we never talk."

"I don't think he talks to *anyone*," Max said.

"I don't know. Mom's right."

"Right about what?"

"She says Dad is too reserved. And if you love someone and he's reserved, he always leaves you wanting more."

The car slowed down and then turned off to the right. We drove down a long, bumpy road. "I probably won't even go to the wedding," Lindsey said.

"Let's change the subject, okay?" Max said. "I'm really getting a headache."

CHAPTER FIFTEEN

It was after ten when we arrived at the cabin. It was set back in the woods overlooking a lake. I couldn't see the water too well, but the air was full of its fresh, damp scent.

The cabin was cozy with white wicker furniture and a stone fireplace in the living room. Max called the bus station as soon as we'd come in.

"The next bus isn't until tomorrow morning," he said. "There's only one bus a day to Portland."

"Oh, no. I'm supposed to take a ferry from Bar Harbor in the morning."

"Can't you take a later ferry?"

"No, they only leave once a day."

"Well, listen, you can spend the night here and I'll take you to the bus tomorrow."

There was nothing else to do. "Thank you. You've been so nice."

"Maybe you'd better call your sister," he said.

"Yes." Max saw me hesitate, and he turned to Lindsey. "Let's see what we can find for dinner." I waited until they went into the kitchen before I called Mattie collect.

"Are you all right, Kate?" Her voice sounded worried.

"Yes, it's just everything is taking longer than expected. I'll be taking the ferry the day after tomorrow."

"Are you sure you're all right? Where are you, anyway?" I said I'd tell her everything when I saw her. "Georgia called."

"She did?"

"Yes. She's in a state. She wants you to call her right away."

"I can't call her now, Mattie."

"I told her you'd be here tomorrow."

"Well, can't you call her and say my bus was delayed? Please."

"She wasn't too happy about the whole thing, Kate." I could only imagine their conversation.

"Look, I can't call her. She'll ask me questions, and I don't want to argue with her just now. Please, tell her I'm safe and I'll speak to her on Monday night. Will you do that?"

There was a long pause. "All right."

"Thank you. I'll see you soon."

"You're okay?"

"Yes, I'm fine."

"All right."

"I'll see you, Mattie," I said, and then hung up.

I went into the kitchen. Lindsey was standing by the stove, pouring soup into a saucepan. She'd changed into a gray sweatshirt and an old pair of jeans. Max had his back to us and was busy rummaging through some cabinets.

"There's tuna," he said. "And a box of saltines—no wait, even better, a box of oyster crackers."

"Did you reach your sister?" Lindsey asked. I think she was only being polite because the cabin was so small that she and Max must have been able to hear me.

"Yes, thanks."

"You probably want to wash up," Max said. "I'll show you the bathroom. I'm afraid the shower's outside, but you can use it in the morning."

I washed my face and hands in the tiny washbasin. The soap had a nice smell. Pears soap.

"Come on, I'll show you around," Max said. There were four rooms to the cabin. The living room, a little kitchen with a counter, and two small bedrooms.

"This was my grandmother," Max said, showing me a picture in an old silver frame. She was a tall, formidable-looking woman with white hair. "Lindsey and I used to spend every August with her. She taught us how to swim, and the three of us used to go canoeing together. Her father built this cabin when she was a girl."

"It's very peaceful here," I said.

"Wait till you see the lake."

"Dinner's ready," Lindsey called.

We ate supper in the living room. Campbell's tomato soup with oyster crackers. Max was going to make a tuna salad, but then he realized that there wasn't any mayonnaise or lettuce.

"It's cold enough to light a fire," Lindsey said.

"Do you want one?" he asked.

"I guess not. I'm going to bed soon. I'm exhausted."

After supper I helped Max wash the dishes, and then he showed me the room where I'd be staying. It was a rectangular room with a child's bureau set between two beds. I opened the window a crack to air things out. Max gave me some clean sheets and a quilt that smelled of mothballs.

Lindsey stuck her head in the door.

"Good night," she said briskly.

"Good night. Does she mind my staying here?" I asked Max.

"No. She's been upset lately because our father is getting married again." I was glad he didn't know I'd been listening in the car. "She doesn't like his girlfriend. She's only twenty-one, his girlfriend," he said.

"Do you like her?"

"I feel sorry for her. She's very shy, and there's

something lonely about her. I think Lindsey would like her if she wasn't marrying our father."

I didn't know what to say.

"You must be tired," Max said.

"I am."

"Think you'll be okay here? Got enough blankets?"

"Yes, I'm fine. Thank you for everything, Max."

"I'm glad to help," he said. "Well, good night, Kate."

"Good night."

I climbed into bed and looked around in the dark. There was a yellow light from a lantern in front of the cabin, and it shone into the room. My sheets smelled fresh and cold. I curled up into a ball and closed my eyes.

The next morning, before the sun rose, Max and I went canoeing. In the blue, smoky light of morning we walked down to the lake at the foot of the road and found his old wooden canoe by the shore. Together we turned it over. There were two paddles inside.

"Are you a good swimmer?" Max said. "Just in case."

"Yes, are you?"

"It's the only sport I'm good at," he said. We inspected the canoe for holes and then carried it down to the water. I took the bow and Max the stern. The boat swayed precariously beneath us as we were seated.

We pushed off into silence, our arms in perfect motion, gliding through the air, splitting the water into music. Smoothly and gracefully we paddled, getting farther and farther away from the shore. On one side of us there were little cabins and houses along the water, and on the other side there was nothing but pine trees. A wind came up behind us, and soon we were sailing.

"Let her go," Max said. "Let her go." I lifted my paddle out of the water and held it across my knee. We were flying now, soaring over the water like a sleek, flying fish. And, for the moment, nothing in the world mattered, I had no past or future, there was only now. And nothing mattered except the rush of the wind and the way the mist around us broke into sparkling light and rose into the day.

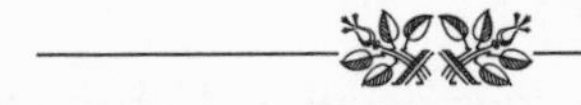

CHAPTER SIXTEEN

"You're kidding, right, Max?"

"I wish I was." The car battery was dead. It had apparently died overnight. Max made the discovery when he went to start the car after breakfast.

"What are we going to do?" I said.

"I'm going to try to get us a lift." He called his nearest neighbor, but she wasn't home. "I'll try Mr. Gunther," he said. He looked up the number and dialed. He was about to hang up when he heard a voice. "Mr. Gunther? Hi, this is Max Wilder. I'm fine, thanks, and you? Good. Listen, I have a great favor to ask of you. My car battery is dead, and I need to take my friend to the bus station in White River Junction. Her bus leaves in half an hour. . . . You will? Thanks very much. Good-bye. He's going to give us a jump start," he said to me. "Don't worry, we'll make it."

Lindsey came out of her room, rubbing her eyes sleepily.

"What's going on?" she asked. Max told her the latest news.

"You're not having much luck, are you?" she said to me, which made me feel awful. "Is there anything for breakfast?" she asked Max.

"There's tea and some biscuits. Come on," he said to me. "Let's wait outside."

"I feel this is all my fault," Max said outside.

"Oh, no, don't say that. Lindsey's right. I haven't had much luck. I looked at my watch. I had twenty minutes to make the bus.

"He should be here any second," Max said, looking up the road. We stood there waiting. Max kicked a stone out of his path. He started to say something and changed his mind. I looked at my watch again.

"Did you hear that?" he said.

"What?"

"I thought I heard a car coming." We both listened again but heard nothing. I was starting to feel sick to my stomach. I couldn't miss this bus. A few more minutes passed. At last an old Ford pickup came riding down the road. Max ran to greet Mr. Gunther.

"Thank you so much for coming," he said. Mr. Gunther smiled at Max, and with his engine still running, he slowly climbed out of his truck. He was a thin, old man in his eighties. His hands were covered with brown freckles.

"How d'you do?" he said to me. "I hear you're in a bit of a pickle."

"Yes, I am." Max got out his cables and started to hook them up to Mr. Gunther's engine.

"Got a bus to catch, eh?"

"Yes."

"Well, don't worry." I tried to smile. "What do you think of my truck?" he asked me. "My wife wants me to paint it cherry red." I told him I liked it the way it was.

"Me, too. My son Alfred bought this truck for my sixtieth birthday. Do you know how long ago that was?" His eyes sparkled. I shook my head.

"Before you were even born," he said, laughing as if it were a great joke. "Before you were even born."

After a few tries Max got his car to start. He took my knapsack and threw it into the backseat.

"Thank you, Mr. Gunther," he said.

"Yes, thank you very much," I said, shaking his hand.

"You're welcome. Have a safe trip now. Don't drive too fast," he said to Max. We tore off down the road.

"Are we going to make it?" I asked.

"I think so." Two miles later we got stuck behind a truck, and I found myself holding my breath, as if not breathing would help us get there faster.

"Maybe the bus won't leave on time," I said.

"Maybe." But when we arrived at White River Junction, the bus had already left. I leaned on Max's car. Tears of frustration were running down my face. Max left the motor running and got out.

"Kate," he said.

"I'm sorry," I said, wiping my eyes. I took a deep breath. "Do you think you could drive me to another bus station?"

"I have a better idea."

"What?"

"I'm going to take you there myself."

"To Portland?"

"No, all the way to Bar Harbor."

"You can't."

"Why can't I?"

"It's too far."

"Look, it's my fault you missed the bus."

"No, it isn't. It's nobody's fault. To tell you the truth, I'm starting to feel as if I weren't meant to go. I mean, first my wallet's stolen and then your car battery dies and . . ."

"Kate, you want to see your sister, right?"

"Yes, but . . ."

"So, I'll get you to the ferry."

"But, Max, it's such a long drive, and anyway, you and Lindsey came up here to have a good time."

"I'll come right back after I drop you off. It's no big deal, really. It'll be fun. Besides, I've never been to Maine."

"I don't know," I said. "It doesn't seem right."

"Why not?"

"I don't want you to feel obligated to me."

"I don't! You'd do the same for me, wouldn't you?"

I shook my head. "I don't drive."

He laughed and said, "Come on, let's go."

We drove to Hanover, and Max cashed a check at the grocery store while I stayed in the car with the engine running. Max didn't dare turn off the motor because he was afraid the battery would die again.

He bought groceries for Lindsey as well as some bread and fruit for us to take on the road.

"I've got to get another battery," he said. "My friend Sam works in a garage up the road."

Sam, a curly-haired man in his late twenties, seemed happy to see Max. "How are you doing?" he said, slapping him on the back. "I was wondering when you'd get up this way. How's Lindsey?"

"She's fine."

"Good. Send her my best."

"This is my friend, Kate," Max said.

"Pleased to meet you," Sam said. He was wearing a pair of gray mechanic's overalls, and I noticed he had a tattoo of an anchor on his forearm.

"What can I do for you?" he asked. Max told him he needed another battery, and Sam said he'd sell him a used one for a good price. While he was installing the battery I heard Sam say to Max, "Is that your girlfriend?"

"No, she's just my friend," Max said. And there was something both defensive and protective in his voice.

When we got back to the cabin, Lindsey was sitting on the front step, drinking a cup of tea.

"What's going on?" she asked. Max told her we'd missed the bus. "I'm going to take Kate to Maine. I'll be back tomorrow night." She didn't look very pleased.

"All right," she said.

"These are for you," he said, carrying a bag of groceries inside. I sat down on the step next to Lindsey and picked up a handful of pebbles. "I'm sorry about all this," I said.

"Don't be silly." We looked out over the lake. The sky was a brilliant summer blue, and the water was like dark green glass. The air smelled sweet, of pine trees.

"This is an incredible place," I said.

"I know. I think it's my favorite spot in the world." Max came out of the cabin with his guitar and a knapsack. He put them in the trunk and patted the car.

"We're all set," he said happily.

She turned to me. "He likes you," she said.

"What?"

"Max. He likes you. I can tell."

I like him, too, I thought. But I didn't say a word to Lindsey.

CHAPTER SEVENTEEN

We had been driving for only an hour when we saw a woman standing in the middle of the road, waving a purple scarf.

Max pulled over a few feet ahead and stopped the car.

"Oh, thank you for stopping," she said. "Hank, look! These lovely children have stopped to help us." She was an elderly woman in her sixties or seventies with very white skin and dyed red hair. She was wearing a lavender sundress that was rather short for someone her age. But her legs were long and shapely. Dancer's legs.

"I'm much obliged," Hank said, looking up from their station wagon. The hood was up and a great cloud of steam was rising into the air.

"Damn thing's overheating again, and I'm low on oil."

"We're on our way to visit our new grandchild," the woman said. "A little boy, nine pounds seven ounces. Now that has to be some baby."

I asked if this was their first grandchild.

"Oh, heavens no. This is our fourth. I love babies, don't you?" Before I could answer, Hank asked if we'd mind giving them a lift to the nearest gas station. "I'd like to call the kids," he said to his wife. "So they don't worry. And I need to get some oil and also some water for the radiator."

Max said he'd be happy to give them a ride.

"You're a darling," the woman said. Hank went to get a plastic container for the water, and then they both climbed into the back of the Volvo.

"I'm Dorothy and this is my husband Hank," the woman said. When she asked us our names, she thought I said Grace, and for the rest of our ride together she and her husband called me Grace. "Perhaps Max and Grace would like a piece of chewing gum" and "Are you in college, Grace?" Max and I grinned at each other, but I never corrected them. I was afraid they'd be embarrassed.

"So, you're interested in music?" Hank said to Max. "Our son Tim is a music lover."

"There's no money in music," Dorothy said. "But you must pursue it anyway just to see if that's what you really want to do."

"Dorothy was an actress," Hank said.

"Really?" I asked.

"Yes, I went to Hollywood when I was nineteen years old. That was before Hank and I were married. He wanted me to stay home and settle down, but I told him if I didn't try this acting business I'd regret it for the rest of my life."

"What happened?" Max asked.

"Well, I lived in Los Angeles for three years, supporting myself as a waitress. I made three pictures the whole time I was there and in every one I played a chorus girl! So, finally I packed up and came home."

Max asked if she had any regrets about her decision.

"Oh, no," she said. "Besides, I'm an easterner at heart. I even like cold weather. When it snows I turn up Sinatra very loud and I'm in heaven!"

"You'd never catch Dorothy down in Florida," Hank said. "She can't bear all that sunshine."

"It destroys the brain cells," she said to me.

Just before we pulled into the gas station Hank drew an old picture from his wallet. "Take a look at this," he said. It was a black-and-white photograph of a line of chorus girls in shorts and tap shoes. "Can you find Dorothy?" he asked, but we couldn't.

"Here she is," he said, pointing to a stunning young woman.

"You look beautiful," I said to Dorothy.

"Thank you. I still have the legs," she said proudly.

"All a woman needs is a good pair of legs and she can get any man in town."

When we dropped them off Hank wanted to pay Max for the lift, but he refused.

"You sure now?"

"I'm sure."

"All right then, drive carefully. And take care of your sweetheart," Hank said to Max, which made me blush. As we drove off I saw Dorothy smiling and waving enthusiastically, as if we were all old friends.

It was late in the afternoon when we arrived in Portland, Maine. We'd been driving for hours, and the day had been incredibly hot. We drove with all the windows down, and the few times we'd stopped and gotten out of the car, I'd felt light-headed and windswept, as if I'd been driving in a convertible.

A few hours north of Portland in Camden, a pretty town with boats along the water, the left rear tire went flat.

"Aren't you glad you came with me?" Max said. "Just think, you could be sitting on an air-conditioned bus right now if it wasn't for me."

"I'd be home right now if it wasn't for you." I handed him the lug wrench and watched as he loosened each bolt and then took off the tire. The back of his T-shirt was soaked with sweat.

"Anyway, I'd rather be here," I said.

"You would?" He stopped working and looked up at me.

"Yes, I . . . I don't feel scared anymore about getting to Nova Scotia." It was true. The panic I'd felt earlier had disappeared, and my whole sense of time had changed. I knew I'd be on the ferry the next morning, and until then, time had taken on an infinite, almost leisurely quality.

"Well, I'm glad," he said. "I mean, I'm glad you're not feeling bad anymore." He finished changing the tire, and then we shared a drink of water from his canteen.

"How about some music?" he said. He took his guitar out of the trunk. It was a light blond Gibson.

"Any requests?" he asked. "Something old, something new?"

"Something old."

"Okay." He played "I've Got a Crush on You," a Gershwin song.

"That's a pretty song," I said when he'd finished.

"Isn't it? Do you sing?" he asked.

"A little."

"Here's another Gershwin," he said, and began to play "Someone to Watch Over Me." I sang along.

There's a somebody I'm longing to see,
I hope that he turns out to be,
Someone to watch over me. . . ."

"You have a great voice!" he said. "A throaty voice."

"Thanks."

"You could be a singer."

"I think about it."

"You should come to New Orleans with me. We could be an act."

I laughed. "You play very well," I told him.

"I'm okay, considering I only started playing a few years ago. I've been told by other musicians that I have potential. But I'm going to need a lot more than potential if I want to make it as a musician."

He played a few more songs, and then he put his guitar away. A bright pink Cadillac sped by with "Just Married" written on the rear window in white paint.

"You have to like pink an awful lot to drive a pink car," he said.

"If I had a car, I'd paint it blue."

"Baby blue?"

"No, deep blue, like this ring," I said, showing him my lapis lazuli.

"You like blue, huh?"

"Yes, I even like the word *blue.* It's a pretty word."

"As opposed to, say, chartreuse or maroon?"

"Exactly. You think I'm silly?"

"No, not silly, *insane.*" I started giggling. I was giddy from traveling.

"All right, get a hold of yourself now, Grace," he said, which made me laugh even harder.

After a while I stopped laughing, and Max said we should probably be on our way. We got back in the car and drove for a few miles in silence. The sun was about to set, and the light was gold.

"Hey, look, there's a fair," I said. We slowed down to look at a crowd gathering in a field off the side of the road. There was a Ferris wheel in the distance and a carousel. Red, white, and blue balloons sailed high above the trees.

"Want to stop?" Max said. "We've got plenty of time. We're only a few hours from Bar Harbor."

"Okay."

A boy in a bright orange T-shirt was directing traffic.

"Park over there," he said, waving us on with a flag. We followed a gray station wagon filled with children, and I felt as if we were part of a caravan.

"Come on," Max said. "I can smell the hot dogs and mustard from here. I'm starving." He took my hand, and we began to run toward the fairground. Smoke from the grills hung in the air in little white clouds. The smell of sizzling meat and mustard mixed with the sweet, sugary scent of cotton candy.

"This is almost as good as the circus," Max said, handing me a hot dog.

"Oh, no, it's much better," I said. "I hate the circus."

"You hate the circus? I don't believe this. I've never heard of anyone hating the circus. Why, it's downright un-American."

I laughed. "I also hate puppet shows and the Three Stooges."

"You're weird, you know that? What about Laurel and Hardy?"

"Oh, I love Laurel and Hardy. Especially Stan, when he cries. Laurel and Hardy, they're not in the same class as the Three Stooges."

"The Marx Brothers?" asked Max.

"Love them."

"Who's your favorite?"

"Groucho. Yours?"

"Harpo. I like the way he puts his leg over people's arms when they go to shake his hand."

"What's your favorite Marx Brothers movie?" I asked.

"Hmm . . . *Duck Soup.*"

"I think mine is *A Night at the Opera.*" He peered at me over his sunglasses. "What's the matter?" I said. The setting sun was in my eyes, and I had to shield them with my hand.

"Nothing," he said, smiling at me. He had a nice smile. It was different from Will's. Max's was quick and warm, and it pulled you in. "Do you like Ferris wheels?" he asked.

"Yes. Don't you?"

"I do," he said. "I really do."

We rode the Ferris wheel twice and ate cotton candy, and Max threw darts at balloons. "This is embarrassing," he said. He'd only managed to pop one balloon. "I mean, it looks so easy."

"Let me try." I got five in a row and won a small stuffed dog with long, floppy ears.

"Here," I said, handing him the dog.

"I'll never live this down," he said.

It was a beautiful evening. The sky was streaked with pink and lavender. Max bought a candy apple for me and a lemonade for himself. A little girl in striped overalls was selling raffle tickets, and Max bought two. We sat down on a stone fence and watched the crowd. A lady in a white dress walked by. The dress had a phosphorescent glow in the coming dark.

"Do you have a boyfriend?" Max asked.

"What?"

"A boyfriend. You. Have one?"

"No. Do you have a girlfriend?"

"Nope. I had one, but we broke up seven months ago."

"Oh." I wondered what his girlfriend had been like and if she was pretty.

"You look so serious," he said. "What are you thinking about?"

Your old girlfriend. But I said, "I like your shirt."

"This old khaki shirt?"

"Yes, it's a nice shirt."

"Thanks. I like it myself." He looked me over. "I like your jacket."

"Thanks." We both laughed.

"You know what I thought when I first saw you in the bus station?"

"No, what?"

"I thought, 'Who is that amazing-looking girl in the Davy Crockett jacket?' "

I smiled. "Yesterday . . . that seems like ages ago."

"Doesn't it? I feel as if we've known each other for years, Kate."

"This has been fun," I said. And then I was suddenly sad because I didn't know if I would ever see Max again.

A silver rocket sped through the sky and disappeared before our eyes.

"A shooting star," Max whispered. He turned to me, and for a moment I thought he was going to kiss me.

"Just think," he said. "Tomorrow night you'll be in Canada."

"I know," I said. But it seemed light-years away. The trees around us stirred in the wind, and I felt the cold, sharp scent of fall wrap around me.

CHAPTER EIGHTEEN

We drove in the dark. The radio played hit tunes from the past. Every now and then the disc jockey came on to announce the next song or reminisce about the last, and his voice was like satin in the night.

"I love this," Max said. "Driving at night, listening to the radio."

"I love it, too." The green lights of the dashboard, the motion of the car, the sound of the wind outside had put me in a trance.

"It's so soothing," Max said. "When I was little, my parents used to take us to my aunt and uncle's place. We'd leave late in the evening to avoid traffic. Lindsey and I would be in our pajamas in the backseat under an old quilt. I just remember the long drive and the calm of it."

I asked him to tell me more about his life down South.

"We had a nice house with a big front yard. My father built us a treehouse, and sometimes Lindsey and I would sleep in it on hot summer nights. It's still there. I walked past our old street a few years ago and it was still there."

He asked me about my parents, and I told him what they had been like. I told him about the house on Eleventh Street and my mother's studio.

"What's your Aunt Georgia like?"

"She's great. You'd like her. She's furious with me right now, but . . ." My voice trailed off. I didn't want to think about how angry Georgia was, so I changed the subject and asked Max if he liked his stepfather.

"He's a nice guy. He looks like Elvis Presley."

"No kidding. Can he sing?"

"Nah, he's got a tin ear." We laughed. "But he used to get stopped all the time when he was young."

"It must be strange to look like a famous person," I said.

"I wouldn't like it."

"Me, either."

"Hey, don't look now, but we are entering the town of Bar Harbor," Max said.

"I don't believe it!"

It was a wealthy-looking New England town, and despite the late hour, it was packed with tourists. There were stores and restaurants open everywhere and couples walked around a pretty village green.

"Let's stop for a minute," Max said. "I'd like to get a hot chocolate or something." We parked the car and found a small store that sold homemade ice cream and penny candies and hot chocolate and coffee and tea. We drank our hot chocolate from Styrofoam cups as we walked around the town, looking in store windows. There were a number of boutiques that were already selling fall and winter clothes.

"I love that it's going to be winter soon," Max said. "I love the winter."

"What about the fall?" That was my favorite season. Red and yellow trees, orange pumpkins, and the sky that deep, intense blue of a Van Gogh painting. To me life seemed more hopeful in the fall, much more so than the spring.

"Oh, the fall's great, too," he said. "But there's something about the winter, the way everything looks covered in snow. I feel protected in the winter."

I imagined us walking down a country road near my house, the air white with frost. I pictured Max in a warm coat with a scarf around his neck. He did not seem the type to wear a hat.

"It's getting windy," he said. "Are you cold, Kate?"

"A little." We walked back to the car.

"Now, I just want to see where the ferry leaves from," he told me. We followed a sign away from the center of town and drove past the dock. "Well, that was easy," he said. We drove out of the town, and Max found a dirt road that he followed for a few miles.

"Where are we?" I said.

"I'm not sure." He pulled over and we both got out and looked around. There were a few stars visible in a dark, hazy sky.

"I see now," I said. We were parked beside an open field. There were no houses in sight.

"This should be all right," Max said. "Let's get out our sleeping bags."

"What sleeping bag?"

"Don't you have a sleeping bag?"

"No."

"I thought you had one in your knapsack," he said.

"No, I didn't bring one. I didn't think I'd need it."

"Oh. Hmm. Well, look, you can have mine."

"No, that's not fair. You take it."

"No. My mother brought me up to be chivalrous, and I can't let her down."

"But you've done too much for me already. Anyhow, we're sleeping in the car, right? I'll just put on some more clothes."

"I'm still giving you the sleeping bag."

"Max." He would not listen to my protests. We both put on layers of shirts and socks and sweaters, and then I draped the sleeping bag over both of us. The only problem was that it didn't unzip all the way, so we could only cover our laps.

Clouds had obscured the stars, and the darkness was almost black.

"It sure gets dark in this part of the world," Max said. "Are you afraid of the dark?"

"Sometimes. If I wake up from a nightmare and my room is pitch dark, I get so scared, I feel paralyzed."

"It's hard to move in that kind of dark," he said. "It feels like everything evil is waiting for you."

"You know what always scared me?"

"What?"

"Tidal waves. When I was little, I read a book called *The Big Wave.* It was about a huge wave destroying this little fishing village in Japan. The image of this colossal wave coming in and washing everything out to sea terrified me."

"You're starting to scare *me,*" he said, and I laughed.

"I don't like volcanoes," he said. "You know, the idea of being trapped in burning lava."

"Doesn't sound too pleasant, no."

"When we studied Pompeii in grammar school, everyone else thought it was neat. But I imagined myself there, trying to run away and being frozen in motion."

"And all these people looking at you thousands of years later."

We both shuddered.

"Let's talk about something else," I said.

"Okay, which *Twilight Zone* scared you the most?"

"No, no," I said. "Something funny, or else I'll never be able to sleep tonight."

"Funny, huh? I can't think of anything funny right now." We both tried to think of something funny, but neither of us could come up with anything.

"Okay, you know which *Twilight Zone* scared me the most?" I said. He shook his head. "The one about the woman who keeps seeing herself. She goes to get on a bus and then she looks up and sees a woman identical to her in the bus window, looking down at her with this mean expression. Oh, *God,* that scared me."

"I never saw that one. The one that got me was the one about the mannequins."

"Oh, yes, I saw that!"

"Maybe we'd better stop now," he said. We stopped talking and listened to the night. There was a slight wind, and we could hear the faint howl of it, along with the sounds of twigs cracking underfoot in the distance.

"It's pretty late," Max said. "Maybe we should try to get some sleep."

"Are you sure about the sleeping bag?"

"Yes, I'm fine. Why don't you take the backseat so you can stretch out a little?"

"Okay." I climbed into the back of the car and crawled into his sleeping bag. Max slipped into the passenger seat and turned off his flashlight.

"'Night," he said.

"Good night."

I don't know how long I lay there, but it seemed like

hours. It had gotten so cold, I had to keep my hands between my legs for warmth.

"Max?" I whispered.

"Yes?" I could tell by his voice that he was wide-awake.

"Aren't you cold?"

"Well, maybe a little," he said through clenched teeth.

"Why don't we share the sleeping bag? We can put it on the ground. We'll both have to sleep on our sides, but at least we'll be warm."

"You think?"

"We can try."

"Okay." He turned on the flashlight and we both got out of the car.

"Let's stay near the car," I said. "It's spooky out here."

"Don't say that!" he said.

We looked around for a good spot.

"How about here?" I said, pointing to the edge of the field.

"Okay."

I took out my poncho and spread it on the ground, laying the sleeping bag over it.

"You get in first, you're bigger," I said. He wiggled his way into the bag, and then I squeezed in beside him.

"All right?" he asked.

"Yes. You?"

"Fine." He turned off the flashlight.

"We can't move, but at least it's warm," he said after a while. I tried to move so my face wasn't smack against his neck, but it was impossible.

"Got enough room?" he asked, and suddenly we both burst out laughing.

"Plenty," I said, and we howled.

"So much room we could play soccer in here," he said.

It was almost impossible to laugh without moving. When one of us even twitched, so did the other. The harder we laughed, the funnier everything seemed.

"I hope we don't have to make a quick getaway tonight," he said, which made me kick my feet as if to pretend I was running.

Finally, after a long time, we both stopped laughing. I pulled up my left arm, the elbow and forearm of which were wedged tight against my chest. With my left index finger I wrote out the word *hi* on Max's back.

"What's that?" he said.

"You have to guess." I drew it again.

"Hi," he said.

"Now what's this?" I asked, drawing a cat.

"An animal. A dog?"

"No, no, a cat." He laughed. "My mother used to draw pictures on our backs with her finger," I told him. "When we couldn't fall asleep or were upset, she'd draw these elaborate pictures and we'd have to guess what they were."

"She sounds nice, your mother," he said.

"She was." We were quiet, and then Max said, "I'm going to sleep now." His voice had a sleepy, droning sound.

"Good night, Grace," he said, which made us both start giggling.

"Good night again," I whispered.

After a while I heard him breathing the slow, rhythmic sounds of sleep. I lay awake in the rich, black dark, listening to the beating of my heart. When I finally saw the faint light of dawn, I closed my eyes. But I did not sleep.

CHAPTER NINETEEN

Early in the morning I felt a sharp stabbing pain in my right calf.

"Max?"

"Hmm?"

"I have to get out."

"What?"

"I have to get out of here." Sleepily he helped me unzip the bag as far as it would go. With great difficulty I wormed my way out. Once on my feet, I ran in little circles, stamping hard on my right foot.

"What's the matter?" he asked.

"Nothing, just a leg cramp. I get them sometimes." I stamped my foot again and again, and slowly the pain subsided as the cramp gave way. Max sat up and watched me. His hair stuck out on one side, and his eyes were puffy from sleep.

"That's one way of waking up," he said. "What time is it, anyway?"

"It's just after six." We rolled up the sleeping bag and washed our faces with the water from Max's canteen. I sat on the hood of the car and brushed my hair.

"I love your hair," he said, reaching out to touch the top of my head. The feel of his hand sent a warm current down my spine. "It's such a lovely color," he said. "A sort of butterscotch."

His hand had moved away, but I could still feel the sensation of it.

"Are you hungry?" he asked.

"Yes."

"I'll make some sandwiches."

We had bread, spread thick with raspberry jam. We ate standing up, side by side, against the car. The sun began to break through the fog.

"I guess we should be on our way soon," he said.

"I guess so." The sun was warm on our faces, and I didn't want to move.

"Kate?"

"Yes?"

"Nothing."

"What is it, Max?" I heard him take a deep breath and then sigh.

"I really like you," he said.

"I really like you, too."

"Well, *that's* good," he said, and reached out and took my hand.

It was a short ride to the ferry. We walked into the terminal holding hands. There were signs and directions written in French and English.

"I'm starting to get butterflies," I said, putting a hand on my stomach.

"Of course you are," said Max. "I'm getting them, too, and I'm not even going." He took out his wallet and handed me some money.

"Thanks, but I don't need this much."

"So, you might get hungry. Anyway, you should always have a little extra money."

"I'll pay you back," I told him. "I promise."

"I know you will," he said. "I *wish* you wouldn't keep saying that."

"I'm going to miss you, Max."

"Me, too. Come on, you'd better get your ticket." He waited on line with me, and then afterward we went outside. On one side of the terminal we saw a line of cars waiting to drive onto the ferry.

"Did you notice the name of the boat?" he asked.

"No, what is it?"

"It's called the *Bluenose.* That must be a good omen, you like the word blue, right?" I smiled. "Hey, you don't have a camera do you?" he asked.

"No."

"Too bad. I wanted to take your picture."

We stood there staring at each other not knowing what to say.

"Hey, I just realized I don't have your address," he said.

"And I don't have yours."

He took out a small notebook. I gave him my address, and then he wrote down his and gave it to me. His handwriting had a funny slant to it.

"I guess I better be going," I said. Neither of us moved.

"Good-bye, Kate."

"Good-bye, Max. Thanks for everything." He shrugged as if to say it's nothing, and then all of a sudden, he pulled me to him and kissed me.

"You're great," he whispered. I slipped my arms around his neck. We kissed again and again. His lips were soft, and his body felt warm, as if he'd been lying in the sun. I could feel my heart taking off like a helium balloon.

"Oh, Kate," he said. "I wish we'd done this sooner."

"Maximillian." I drew him close and blinked my eyelashes against his cheek. "That's a butterfly kiss," I said. "So you don't forget me."

"Oh, I couldn't forget you." He looked at me and smiled. And I thought how slow and stuck my life had seemed just a few weeks ago, and how everything was moving so fast now.

Somewhere in the distance a voice called out to a friend, "Hurry up or you'll miss the boat."

"You better go," he said. We held each other tight.

A haze of morning light surrounded us, silvery and luminous.

"Kiss me again!" I said. We kissed once more a deep, bottomless kiss. I felt the light, quick beat of his heart. "Good-bye!" I whispered and then I turned and hurried toward the ferry.

The smell of the boat hit me right away—a humid, briney smell of weathered wood and ocean air. I climbed to the upper deck. The boat was crowded with families with young children and students with backpacks. I looked for Max down below, but I could not find him.

Suddenly the fog horns were blowing. I ran over to another railing. It was drizzling now, and the hills on land were a pale gray, the same color as the sea. To one side there were a number of little islands jutting out of the water with nothing on them but green trees. I felt the slow, strong motion of the boat beneath my feet as it moved away from the harbor.

"Good-bye, good-bye!" People were shouting and waving at the shore. And at last I saw Max standing near his car. When he saw that I'd seen him he saluted me, and I saluted back.

I watched him drive off in his old green car. He turned right at the top of the road. And then he was gone.

CHAPTER TWENTY

About twenty minutes out to sea a dense fog encircled the boat, and most of the people who were outside went downstairs. I had my poncho so I didn't mind the damp, wet deck. I leaned over the railing and stared at the water churning below. The ocean was hypnotic. In the distance it was a steel gray, but up close to the boat it was pale green and foamy white.

"If you jumped off the ship do you know what would happen?"

I turned around and saw a little boy standing next to me.

"No, what?"

"You'd get sucked underneath and chopped up by the propellers."

"That sounds horrible."

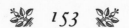

"My name is Clifton," the boy said. He was wearing a red plastic raincoat and a large sou'wester.

"Kate. Is this your first boat trip?" I asked.

"Yes. The *Bluenose* is not as big a ship as I imagined it would be, but I'm not disappointed, are you?"

"No, I'm not." His eyes were large and dark in his thin, little face. "Are you cold, Clifton?" I asked. His teeth were chattering.

"Just a little. You know what I used to think?" he said putting one foot up on the lowest rung of the railing.

"What?"

"I used to think if I fell overboard I could swim along beside the boat. But then my father told me I'd get dragged under." I looked around to see if his father was nearby, but I didn't see anyone else around.

"I like the way the boat smells don't you?" he said.

"Yes, I do."

"Clifton!" a voice called out. "I've been looking for you everywhere!" We turned to see a small woman in a tan raincoat. Her face was slightly green and she was gripping onto the railing. "I have to go now," Clifton told me, touching my arm briefly with his small, cold hand.

"Good-bye," I said.

"Good-bye."

After he left I walked around the boat, but then I started to feel hungry so I went inside. Downstairs there was a gift shop and a tacky-looking lounge, and farther down the corridor was a buffet room and a snack bar as well. The buffet room was too expensive, so I went to the snack bar and bought myself a sandwich and a cup of tea and sat down at a table. The room was crowded and noisy, and it smelled of cigarette smoke. I ate my cheese-and-tomato sandwich, which was soggy, and drank my tea. I saw a girl with long braids standing a few feet away, holding a tray of food. She was looking for a place to sit down. Her eyes caught mine and I smiled. She nodded at my table, and I nodded back.

"It's so crowded in here," she said, sitting across from me. She unwrapped a ham sandwich and opened a small container of milk.

"My name is Vanessa," she said, reaching across the table to shake hands.

"Kate."

"I noticed you up on deck earlier. I think we were the only two people outside."

"It's so smoky in here," I said.

"This isn't half as bad as it can be," she said. "I've done this trip twice this summer."

"Do you have family in Nova Scotia?" I asked.

"My lover lives in Yarmouth."

The word *lover* took me by surprise. In truth it shocked me. I didn't know anyone who said "my lover" this or "my lover" that. There was a boldness about it that I admired. To say "my lover" was to come right out and say "the person I make love with."

"Is he Canadian?" I asked. *Your lover.*

"Yes, he was born on Prince Edward Island. Have you been there?"

"No."

"Oh, you should go. It's so pretty. It's where *Anne of Green Gables* took place. Did you ever read that book when you were a kid?"

"Yes, I loved it. And *Anne of Avonlea*, too."

I watched as Vanessa finished her sandwich and then took out a paper bag from her coat pocket.

"Have an oatmeal cookie," she said.

"Thank you."

After eating we both wandered through the boat. There were people having cocktails in the lounge, and I wondered how anyone could drink so early in the day. I said this to Vanessa.

"Oh, people love to get looped on boats. It passes the time."

We went upstairs and out on deck. The fog had lifted quite a bit, but it was still cold. We finished the rest of the cookies, and then Vanessa said she needed to sleep.

"I've been up for twenty-four hours. I had to drive all night to make it to the ferry on time." She found a bench and stretched out, using her knapsack as a pillow.

"See you later," she said.

I found an enclosed area with a green cement floor and about fifteen empty canvas chairs. I sat down and opened my knapsack, looking for my diary. There was

Max's khaki shirt! He must have put it in when I wasn't looking. I laughed aloud. The shirt smelled of him, a mixture of outdoors and a sweet boy scent. I took out my diary and wrote,

> Dear Max,
> I'm sitting on the *Bluenose* ferry, somewhere out in the Atlantic Ocean. I love you.

The "I love you" just slipped out. Could I love someone I'd only known for three days? Why not? I thought of Will and how despite all the years I'd known him, I'd never really loved him the way I loved Max. And that was odd because I'd wanted Will to love me for so long and now I didn't care. I wrote:

> I just found your shirt. Thank you. What a great surprise. I'm so glad to have something of yours to keep. I miss you.

I held his shirt against my face and thought about the last time we'd kissed, just before I walked away. When we'd kissed then everyone had disappeared, and it seemed as if we were all alone in the world.

I took off my jacket and my poncho and slipped on his shirt. It would always remind me of Max and of the end of summer.

At the first sight of land, everyone came out on deck. In my fantasies I'd pictured Yarmouth as an old boating town, quaint and beautiful like Nantucket.

But this harbor was larger and more modern than I'd expected, and there were a number of cold, institutional buildings.

I walked down the covered walkway and followed a crowd of passengers into the customs building. I waited on line until it was my turn, and then I was questioned by a kind-faced woman. She asked me my name and place of birth and why I was coming to Canada. I told her I was here on holiday to see my sister. It was all very quick, and afterward when I walked outside, I felt a bit dazed.

In the distance I saw a wire-mesh gate, and behind it there were many cars. I walked outside the gate and looked around. Mattie had told me to meet her at the gate. All around me people were greeting one another. I took off my poncho and stuffed it into my knapsack. I brushed my hair and thought of braiding it but decided not to. I straightened my clothes as best I could. And then I waited for Mattie.

CHAPTER TWENTY-ONE

Almost everyone had gone by the time I saw an old, navy blue Mustang coming my way. It drifted to a stop, and then Mattie was getting out and walking toward me. Her hair was cut short to her chin with bangs, like an Oriental doll. The same beautiful face.

"You cut your hair," I said.

She smiled at me. I felt the wind stir around us. Her hand brushed against her hair as if by accident, and then she put her hands in her pockets.

"You don't look twelve anymore," she said. I shook my head and tried to smile, but all of a sudden I was crying. She put her arms around me and held me close.

"Oh, Kate, I'm so glad you've come." We held each other in a tight embrace. She smelled the same, of lavender soap. *My sister.*

"The jacket looks good," she said. "Come here, I've got something to show you." She took my hand and pulled me over to the car. I peered inside. Lying fast asleep in a car seat was a dark-haired baby.

"Oh, Mattie!"

"Her name is Katharine," she said with a big smile. "I call her Kit." I started crying again.

"She's beautiful," I whispered. "How old is she?"

"Ten months. You're old Auntie Kay now," she said, squeezing my arm.

The drive was quiet. The baby slept, and Mattie and I spoke in low voices. We drove along the coast, through small towns with barnlike houses, painted peach or bright green or white with delft-blue roofs. Fresh, clean laundry stretched across clotheslines, flapping dry in the wind. The houses and terrain were foreign to me, doleful and lonely. There were no people out on the roads, no signs of life beyond the houses.

"I live in a pretty place," she said, as if reading my thoughts. "There are apple orchards across the road and a view of the water."

"How far is it?" I asked.

"Not far now, a little less than an hour from here. Are you tired?"

"No, I'm fine." I watched her as she drove. She wore jeans and a forest-green cotton sweater she must have knit herself. She looked older and a little more tired, but she was still extraordinarily beautiful.

"Dean's gone," she said, not quite looking at me, keeping her eyes on the road.

"Gone where?"

"Just gone. He left when the baby was three months old."

"Oh, Mattie."

"It doesn't matter now. It was terrible at first. But it doesn't matter anymore."

I turned to look at the baby. She was wearing blue overalls and a pink shirt. She slept with her head to one side and her mouth slightly open. Her hair was black and see-through fine. Dean's dark-haired baby.

I leaned back in the seat and looked out the window. Just this morning I'd said good-bye to Max, and now I was in Nova Scotia with my sister and her baby. My niece. I thought of Max waving good-bye to me, of the feel of his lips when we kissed. So much had happened.

Mattie turned to look at me, and I smiled.

"What a time I've had getting here," I said.

"A real journey?"

"Yes, a real journey."

We drove on and the landscape changed. It was lush now and not quite so desolate. We came into the town of Annapolis Royal, a pretty green place with Victorian houses and the pleasant feel of history.

"I'm just a few miles from here," she said. "We're in farm country now." Sheep grazed in the pastures, and all along the road there were little wildflowers of yellow and lavender. Across the road there were apple orchards on sloping hills leading down to the water. We turned right, up a steep hill, on top of which sat an old white house.

"This is it," Mattie said.

I watched as she unstrapped the baby and carried her from the car. The baby was stirring now; she opened her eyes and looked at me. "That's your Auntie Kay," Mattie said softly. "Your namesake. She's come all the way from Massachusetts to see you." The baby had very black eyes, and her skin was the color of a pale peach.

"Hello," I said. I reached out slowly and kissed one of her hands. She blinked at me.

"You're all wet," Mattie said, patting her behind. "I've made muffins for us, and I have black currant tea," she said. "Aren't you hungry?"

"Yes," I said. "Very." I followed them up the path and into the house.

The house was old and worn and a bit stark, but Mattie had done her best to make it bright. There was a blue-and-white rag rug on the living-room floor and a rocking chair and an old couch with a quilt thrown over it. The kitchen was square and small with pretty pots of flowers and plants on the windowsill. Mattie's room was spartan compared to her old room back home. Gone were all the little odds and ends. There was a double bed with a down quilt, a red-painted bureau, and a low bookshelf crammed tight with books. On top of the bookshelf was a photograph of our parents.

"You can sleep in the living room or with the baby," Mattie said. "If you don't mind."

"I don't mind."

"She has the nicest room, anyway. Here, you can see for yourself." The baby's room was very sunny with windows on three sides. The floor was painted buttercup yellow, and the crib was white with a mobile of little teddy bears hanging above it. Everything looked fresh and newly painted. There was a bureau, which served as a changing table, a plastic hamper, and a shelf with stuffed animals and toys. It had that nice smell that babies' rooms have. The smell of freshly laundered clothes, baby lotion, and baby oil. Opposite the crib was a single bed with a gingham bedspread.

"This is perfect," I said, sitting on the bed. Mattie changed the baby's diaper and dressed her in a clean pair of pants.

"You're all dry now," she said, kissing her cheek. She lifted the baby onto her hip. "Come on, I'll show you the rest of the house."

I followed them up a narrow flight of stairs. "This is where I work," she said, opening a door to her right. It was a large, rectangular room with white walls and dark wood floors. There was a sewing machine by a window and, in the corner, a glass cabinet filled with yarn. A long desk made from an old door was pushed against a wall. Above the desk was a bulletin board covered with patterns and photographs of stylish models. In the middle of the room was a long pole suspended from the ceiling by two chains. This was where Mattie hung her creations. A series of patchwork dresses hung from the pole on wooden hangers.

"Those are for the spring," she said. "I make them for a boutique in Halifax. I also make sweaters and hats," she said, opening up a closet door. Twenty or more sweaters were folded neatly on shelves. In a round straw basket beneath them was a pile of hats and gloves. The sweaters were bulky and warm, made with thick, soft wool. I'd have known they were Mattie's anywhere. They were her colors: forest greens, deep blues, mauves, and lavenders.

"I also have an idea for a line of babies' clothes, called Fabulous Babies. I'm going to work on it this winter."

"This is great, Mattie. You make such beautiful things."

"How about some tea now?" she asked. "We can have it in the garden."

On the way downstairs I asked what was in the room across from her workroom.

"Nothing. It was Dean's darkroom. There's nothing in it now."

I played with the baby while Mattie made the tea, and then I helped carry the cups and saucers out into the backyard. We sat on a blanket on the grass. Most of the land around us was overgrown with tall grass and weeds. But Mattie had made two gardens on either side of the backyard. One was a vegetable garden with tomatoes, lettuce, peppers, and cucumbers. The other was a tiny flower garden of roses and impatiens and daisies.

"Does Georgia still have her roses?" she asked.

"Oh, yes. They were incredible this year. Yellow and pink, the best yet."

"She taught me a lot about flowers. It's funny. She couldn't cook a decent meal if she tried, but she could plant a garden full of beautiful roses."

The black currant tea was delicious and soothing, and the muffins were sweet and warm. The baby sat on Mattie's lap and drank milk from a cup. All of a sudden I felt a great weariness come over me.

"I think I'll take a nap now," I said.

"Why don't you go lie down in my room? That way the baby won't wake you up."

"Okay," I said, starting to clear my plate.

"Leave that," she said. "I won't let you sleep too long, otherwise you won't be able to sleep tonight."

"All right," I said. I turned to go, and then I stopped.

"I'm really here, aren't I?" I asked.

"Yes," she said quietly. "You're really here."

CHAPTER TWENTY-TWO

I woke up to the sound of classical music. The room was very dark, and for a moment I didn't know where I was. I heard the sound of someone rattling around in a kitchen. The sounds of a pot being laid down on a stove, a drawer being opened and shut. I closed my eyes and opened them again. *Mattie's house.*

I turned, very slowly, over to my side. My sleep had been so deep and dark, I felt as if I'd been unconscious. I heard a high, sweet voice say, "Ma-ma," and I remembered with surprise that there was a baby in the house. *Mattie's baby.* Lying still in the dark, in between sleeping and waking, I listened to my sister moving around.

When we were little, Jay and I would lie in bed, listening to our parents talk to one another in the kitchen. They would drink coffee or red wine and discuss their day. We could always catch a phrase or two or recognize the name of one of their friends. But mostly we didn't listen to what they said as much as to how they said it. The cadence of their voices was like the ebb and flow of an ocean, a murmuring in the dark. The light from the kitchen spilled under our door as we lay safe and warm in our beds. And I never thought back then that there would be an end to this comfort, that I would turn eight and lose them forever. I never thought there would be anything but that peace.

I sat up slowly and swung my legs over the side of the bed. After a moment I stood up and turned on a light. I stared at my reflection in the mirror. I looked bewildered, a ghost of myself. My body felt sluggish. I shuffled into the kitchen.

"There you are," Mattie said. "I was going to wake you in a little while."

The baby sat in her high chair, staring at me with a solemn face.

"Kate, you look as if you're still asleep," Mattie said.

"I am. I think I'll take a bath. I have to get out of these clothes."

"I'll run it for you," Mattie said, "if you keep an eye on the baby." The baby watched Mattie leave the room, and then she turned to me. The tray on her high chair was covered with carrots and potatoes. She carefully picked up a piece of carrot and offered it to me.

"Thank you," I said, taking it from her soft, chubby

little hand. I popped it in my mouth. "Delicious," I said. Immediately she picked up a piece of potato and held it out to me.

"Oh, I think, I'm full now. You eat it," I told her. Without taking her eyes from my face she dropped the potato. It fell onto the floor and began to roll under the table. I bent down on all fours to pick it up. With great interest the baby leaned over the side of her high chair to watch me.

"What are you two up to?" Mattie said, coming in. She carried a chenille robe over one arm. "Here, Kate," she said. "You can wear this while you're here. We can wash your clothes tomorrow."

I waved good-bye to the baby and made my way down the hall. In the distance I could hear the water running for the bath, a great rushing noise like a waterfall. It was an old-fashioned bathroom with an oval sink and a tub with claw feet. The walls were covered with a faded floral wallpaper. Mattie had laid out a clean towel and a new bar of soap. I held the soap to my nose. Cucumber.

On the wall above the sink was a framed photograph of Mattie and Jay and me when we were kids. We were sitting in a row with towels wrapped around our heads like turbans. One of Jay's front teeth was missing.

All of a sudden I missed Jay. I wished he were here with Mattie and me. I wished the three of us were all together and that we'd never been estranged.

Mattie and I had black bread and vegetable soup for dinner and cold, boiled potatoes and a green salad from the garden.

"Everything tastes so good," I said. I was starving. The robe Mattie had loaned me was soft and cozy against my skin. My hair smelled of baby shampoo.

"Feeling better?" Mattie asked.

"Yes."

"There's nothing like a hot bath," she said.

"Nothing."

The baby sat near us on the floor. She was playing with a wooden spoon and three plastic pots. Every once in a while when she became excited, her voice went up like the trill of a bird.

"Who does she look like?" I said.

"She's got Dean's coloring and his dark hair."

"I know, but what about her features—her eyes and her mouth . . ."

"I think they're her own."

"You're right."

After supper Mattie put Kit to bed and we cleaned up the kitchen. I washed the dishes, and Mattie got down on her hands and knees with a sponge and scrubbed the floor around the baby's high chair.

"I do this three times a day," she said. "You wouldn't believe how much food ends up here." She looked up at me and smiled, and I noticed how tired she looked.

"You look like you're ready for sleep, Matt," I told her.

"Soon," she said. "Pretty soon. It's nice to have you here, Kate."

"For me, too." We smiled at each other. I didn't tell her how quietly shocking it was to be there. How, after all the time apart, it took my breath away to see my sister as a young woman with a baby, to see her pretty but isolated house, to see her without a man to adore her. To see her alone.

I sat down at the kitchen table as Mattie put a kettle on the stove and finished watering her flowers. She brought out two cups and saucers and then came and sat down opposite me.

"When do you have time to sew?" I asked her.

"Oh, I'm lucky because Kit naps in the day. And then I work at night, too. I mostly work at night. I'd be sunk if she wasn't such a good baby."

"Do you ever have any help?"

"No. I can't afford it."

The kettle began to whistle and she made the tea. It was very hot, and we drank it slowly in little sips.

"You know, you look like Mom," she said.

"Oh, no, she was beautiful."

"And you look like her. Your hair, your figure."

"I have something of Mom's for you," I said. I found the letter in my knapsack and handed it to her.

She looked at it curiously, her greengage eyes widening as she read it. When she looked up, her eyes were filled with tears.

"Georgia gave it to me," I said. "I thought you should have it."

"Thank you. It's funny," she said, "but when I was pregnant, and then right after I had the baby, I missed Mom terribly. I still do. Every time Kit gets another tooth or learns something new, I think of Mom. We were never close the way I was with Dad, but even so, she's the one I miss."

I wondered if it ever ended, that terrible yearning for our parents. It wasn't like that all the time, not even most of the time, but still there were moments when we would do anything to have them back again, moments when the fact of their death was still unbearable.

"That's Mom's ring, isn't it?" Mattie said, picking up my hand delicately in her own.

"Yes."

"It suits you. These garnets were hers," she said, pointing to the small red stones in her ears. "I'm going to give them to Kit one day."

We finished our tea, and then Mattie said she was going to bed.

"Are you sure you'll be all right in Kit's room?"

"Fine. I prefer it to the living room."

"She likes you," she said.

"The feeling is mutual."

"Do you have everything you need?" she asked.

"Yes."

"Well, good night, then, Kate."

" 'Night."

I waited for her to wash up and go to bed before I picked up the phone. Georgia answered on the first ring.

"Where are you?"

"I'm at Mattie's."

There was a brief pause, as if she were just catching her breath, and then, "I'm absolutely furious with you," she said. I didn't say anything. "How could you do this, Kate?"

"I didn't want to do it this way, Georgia. I told you I wanted to see Mattie, but you wouldn't let me."

"So you ran away."

"I'm not running away."

"When are you coming home?"

"I'm not sure. In a week or so."

"How will you get here?"

"I'll take the boat and then a bus."

"What's she doing in Canada, anyway?"

"She likes it here." I didn't mention the baby. "How's Jay?"

"He's fine. He has a new job waiting tables three nights a week."

"What about the pharmacy?"

"He still works there days."

"Is he home?"

"No, he's working."

We were both silent, and then I said, "Georgia, I'm very sorry if I hurt you." She didn't answer me for a long time.

"You had me worried to death," she said at last.

"I'm sorry."

"Come home soon, Kate," she said. She sounded as if she were about to cry.

"I will. I promise. I'll call you in a few days."

"All right," she said, and then she hung up.

I turned out the kitchen lights and opened the door to the baby's room. There was a Bambi night-light on near her crib. I stood there for a moment, watching her sleep. She lay on her stomach, her behind raised up slightly in the air. I adjusted her flannel blanket so that her feet were covered. And then I got into bed and went to sleep.

CHAPTER TWENTY-THREE

"Dee, dee, dee." I opened my eyes and saw Kit standing up in her crib, doing little knee bends and chattering to herself. When she saw that I was awake, she got very excited and lifted her knees up high, as if she were marching.

"Hi, Kit Kat," I said, going over to the crib.

"Da, da, da."

"Oh, you smell so good," I said, picking her up. I talked to her in whispers as I changed her diaper, a stream of silly, rhythmic, nonsensical talk that babies bring out in me.

"Hi there, pretty girl. You are a lovely baby. Lovely, lovely little Kit." I kissed her belly, which made her laugh, and then I dressed her in a pair of cotton pants and a T-shirt with snaps on one side of the shoulder. Mattie came in, in her nightgown. Her hair was tousled, and her eyes were half closed.

"Go back to bed," I said. "You look terrible."

"I didn't sleep too well."

"So go back to sleep. I'll take care of the baby. I know how, you know. I used to baby-sit for a little boy."

"But I don't want to burden you."

"It's not a burden, it's a pleasure. Go on."

"All right. She can have an egg for breakfast or some of that baby cereal mixed with apple juice and a banana, too, if she wants."

"Fine."

"You sure?"

"Positive."

"Okay, thanks."

I scrambled an egg for Katharine and cut it up into pieces and put it on the tray of her high chair. I made a pot of coffee and ate a slice of black bread with butter and jam. The kitchen was sunny and warm. The baby ate her egg, and I gave her some juice from her tin cup. She seemed happy to see me, and she banged her cup against the tray over and over.

Afterward we went outside, and I carried her on my hip as I walked around. The trees around us were lush with leaves, but still there was something forlorn about the place.

I sat down on the back steps and gave the baby my bracelets to play with. Later Mattie came out with two cups of coffee.

"I haven't slept this late since before she was born."

"It's good for you." She sat down beside me. "We had a nice time this morning," I said. "She's such a happy baby."

"I know. In the mornings, when I go into her room and she's standing up in her crib, smiling, I can't believe my luck."

We both watched as the baby pulled herself up without holding on to anything. She stood there for a moment, as if she were deciding to take a step, and then she sat back down.

"Changed your mind about walking?" Mattie said, sweeping her up in her arms. "She's so close to walking by herself."

"She's a smart girl, " I said. "I hope I have a girl one day."

"How many kids do you want?" she asked.

"Oh, three."

"Do you? They're a lot of work."

"But it's worth it, isn't it?"

"Yes. Even raising a child alone, as hard as it is, it's worth it."

In the afternoon Mattie and I took the baby for a long walk in her stroller. "It's beautiful here, Mattie, but it seems so lonely. Who do you see?"

"I don't see anyone, really. Except the people I do business with."

"Don't you have any friends?"

"They turned out to be Dean's friends. Oh, there's

a woman, I see sometimes, Abby Redfield. She's nice, a poet. But she lives about a hundred miles away, so I don't get to see her very often."

"Doesn't it make you crazy? Not seeing anyone?"

"It did at first, especially after Dean left. But then I became sort of used to it."

"Do you ever think of coming back to Stockbridge?"

"Sure. But I don't have anything set up there, as far as making a living. And I have the house here—I own it. That's one thing Dean left me. And now I'm just beginning to get a business going."

"But don't you miss . . . ?"

"What?"

"I don't know, going to the movies, going dancing. You used to like to dance."

"I could go to the movies if I wanted. There's a university in Wolfville; that's not too far from here. It's a nice place, and there are lots of young people there. As far as dancing, well, I don't know anyone to dance with." We walked down to an old church. Then the baby started fussing and Mattie said she was hungry.

We took the baby home and gave her a snack, and then we put her down for a nap. Mattie had washed my clothes in the morning and hung them out to dry. They smelled of fresh air and sunlight. I took them off the clothesline, and then I set up the ironing board in the kitchen. Mattie went upstairs to work on her dresses.

In the evening we had gazpacho for dinner, and then I took the baby out for another walk so Mattie could work. After the baby went to bed Mattie and I sat in the living room and listened to the radio. Mattie was knitting a pale yellow baby's hat.

"Do you still like to sing?" she asked.

"Yes."

"That's good. I used to be terribly jealous of your voice."

"Were you?" I had always thought Mattie had so much that it was hard to imagine her being jealous of anyone, especially me.

"I can hardly carry a tune," she said, "and you, you can make people stop and listen when you sing."

"Thanks."

"How is Jay?" she asked.

"He's fine. He wants to be a doctor."

"I didn't know he was interested in medicine."

"He's always been." It irritated me that she didn't remember that about Jay. "Don't you remember the time I cut my foot and there was glass in it and Jay took it out and bandaged it for me? And when we went to the doctor later, he said that Jay did a great job, even if he was only nine."

"I don't remember."

"You don't remember?"

"There are a lot of things I don't remember."

"Do you remember the time Mom got something in

her eye and Jay was the only one who could get it out?"

"No," she said.

Mattie was hopeless.

"You just don't want to remember," I said.

"Why are you mad at me?"

"It just seems convenient not to remember."

"I can't help it if my memory isn't as good as yours."

But it seemed to me that her forgetting was deliberate, a way of making the past insignificant.

"I'm going to bed now."

"Kate?"

"What?"

"I do remember some things."

I shrugged. I didn't want to talk to her anymore.

"I remember Eleventh Street."

"I went there with Jay," I said coldly.

"You did? When?"

"A few weeks ago. We walked by the house."

"How did it look?"

"Oh, you know, the same."

"Did you see Andy?"

"Yes. And Will."

"Will's in New York?"

"Going to graduate school."

"How is he?" she asked.

Still in love with you. "Fine " I said.

"We broke up in such a bad way," she said.

"Not bad for you."

"It wasn't easy for me."

"Yeah, but you had Dean."

"Good ol' Dean," she said with a short laugh. "So tell me, how is Will?" she asked, changing the subject.

"I told you, he's fine. He likes New York."

"Does he have a girlfriend?"

"I don't know. He seems to know a lot of people. Do you still care about Will?" I asked.

"Of course. I love Will but not like that."

"Like what, then?"

"It's hard to explain. I don't think Will ever understood me. I know he thinks he did, but he didn't."

"Sure he did! He loved you, Mattie. Maybe you don't like people to love you."

"Loving someone and knowing them are two different things. He wanted me to be who *he* wanted me to be. Anyway, he thought I was someone else. I can't explain it better than that."

"You didn't have to be so mean to him," I said.

I felt as if I were talking through Will, like a medium. When I told my sister she didn't have to be so mean to Will, I meant she didn't have to be so mean to *me.* And when I said, "Will loved you," I wanted to say, "*I* love you."

"Oh, Kate," she said. "You think everything is black or white. To you I was bad and Will was good.

It's more complicated than that."

"How?"

"I loved Will. I still do. But he was all over me. It was too much. He acted like he couldn't breathe without me."

I didn't know what to say. I'd never had anyone love me like that. I'd always seen Will's love for my sister as romantic, but to Mattie it was irritating.

"I don't know, Mattie," I said. "You can be so hard sometimes."

"You don't understand."

"What? What don't I understand?"

"What it's like for people to expect so much from you," she said, her voice rising. "It's like having to win a gold medal at the Olympics, not just once, but every time."

"Nobody's talking about gold medals. I'm talking about being decent and kind and unselfish. I'm talking about not running away." We stared at one another.

"I did what I had to do," she said.

"No. You did what you *wanted* to do!"

"I can't help it if you see it like that."

"That's how I *see* it, because that's how it is!" I walked out of the room and went outside. It was freezing, but I did not want to be in the same house with Mattie. I hated her then.

"Kate," she said, coming to the door.

"Go away," I said.

I waited until I heard her go to bed before I came back inside. Celia and Jay had been right: I was crazy to have left home, crazy to have come all this way. Mattie would never change. She'd always be selfish, always doing what she wanted, no matter what the cost. "I can always leave tomorrow," I whispered to myself. But there was little comfort in that thought. And after all my effort I was sorry I'd come.

CHAPTER TWENTY-FOUR

"Have some breakfast," Mattie said.

It was a rainy morning. The baby was sitting in her playpen, teething on a red rubber ring.

"Ah, ah, ah," she said, catching my eye.

"Ah, ah, ah," I said back.

"I've made oatcakes from an old Nova Scotian recipe," Mattie said, coaxing. The kitchen smelled of coffee and freshly baked biscuits. There were daisies on the table.

"Don't be mad, Kate," she said.

I had awakened with a sense of dread. My fight with Mattie made my trip seem a failure, a small adventure for nothing. I wished Max were with me. I longed to kiss him again, to feel his arms around me. I had not washed his shirt because I was afraid of losing his smell. But then, when I put it on, the scent of him made me miss him more and I became weepy.

I had expected Mattie to be angry, to freeze me out the way she did when I was little. But, instead, I could see that she was trying to patch things up.

"What do you want me to do?" she asked. "I can't change the past."

"I know."

She sat down beside me. Her face was pale and tight from lack of sleep. "I don't want us to fight," she said.

"I can't pretend about how I feel."

"No."

"I don't know, Mattie, it just seems . . ."

"What?"

"Everything is always on your terms."

"How?"

"Well, you run away, and no one knows where you are for *three* years, and then you get back in touch when *you* want to. Never mind about the rest of us."

"It's not like that."

"Yes, it is," I said quietly. "You've always done things your way."

"Why did you come?"

"Because I wanted to see you."

"I wanted to see you, too, Kate. You know that."

"Yes, but would you have come to see me? If I had asked you, would you have come?"

"I don't know." She was being honest. And her honesty hurt. "Listen, it wouldn't be easy for me to come home."

"Because of Georgia?"

"Yes."

I shook my head. "I don't understand, Mattie. I never have."

"If I came home now, Kate, I'd be coming home as a failure."

"Why? That's not true. And Georgia wouldn't see it like that. She's your family. She loves you, Mattie."

"Well, anyway, what's past is past," she said. "I'm living here now." The baby started crying, and Mattie picked her up. "My life is here."

We did not talk anymore about Georgia that day. And I did not think of leaving just yet.

That afternoon I helped my sister pack up her sweaters and dresses to be sent to Halifax the next day. We sat on the floor of her workroom wrapping them carefully in tissue paper.

"I'm so late," she said. "I was supposed to send these out last month." We sealed the boxes with strapping tape and took them downstairs. The sun had come out, but still the air was cold and damp.

"Come on, I'll make some cocoa," she said. "It will help take the chill out of the day."

The cocoa was rich and sweet, made with fresh cream. We took our cups into Mattie's room and sat on her bed. She pulled a black leather album from her bookshelf. It was full of pictures of Kit. On the first page was a picture of Mattie, nine months' pregnant.

"That was taken two weeks before Kit was born."

"Look at your breasts," I said.

"Torpedoes."

"Dolly Parton," I said, and we both laughed. I looked at a picture of Kit when she was two days old. "She looks like a little doll," I said.

"I know. She was seven pounds at birth, and she looked like a peach. She never had that old, wrinkled face that some babies have." I realized that she'd probably never shown these pictures to anyone.

"What was the birth like?"

"It was hard. Terrible. I was in labor for twenty hours. At the end it turned out that her head was stuck, so the doctor had to reach in with his hand and turn it. After that she popped out."

"Was Dean there?"

"Yes. He was there the whole time. That's why I couldn't understand how he could leave us three months later. He had seen his own child being born, but that didn't seem to make a difference."

"Where did he go?"

"Vancouver. I'm not sure where he is right now."

"Does he send you money at least, for the baby?"

"He sends what he can. He's spent most of his inheritance. It wasn't very much to begin with. I don't think it's dawned on him yet that he's going to have to get a job. The last time we spoke, he told me I should sell the house and move back to Massachusetts." She stood up suddenly.

"What did you see in Dean?" I asked.

"You never liked him, did you?"

"No one did."

"Well, whatever I saw in him I certainly don't see it now."

"But what was it? It had to be something strong, or else you would never have left."

"It *was* strong. There was chemistry between us. A great physical attraction. Everything seemed charged and exciting when he was around. And then he was older than me, and I guess I liked that. All I remember is, in the beginning, I couldn't think of anything but him."

She put the album away and went into the kitchen to prepare dinner. Shortly after the baby woke up from her nap, Mattie fed her and gave her a bath. I stood in the doorway of the bathroom as she was drying her on her lap with a soft, white towel. The baby was crying because she had not wanted to get out of the water.

"It's okay, Kit," Mattie said. "You'll have another bath tomorrow." The baby kicked her feet and waved her arms in a fury. And Mattie tried wearily to comfort her.

I slipped away before they could see me and went for a walk. The sun had set, turning the sky rose, and down below, the apple orchards were bathed in pink and yellow light.

I walked until a violet twilight descended, and then I turned back toward her house. In the distance, through a light in the window, I could see Mattie putting Kit to bed. The house looked stark white against the evening sky, and behind it on the hill to the left, I could see the pale blue sheets on the clothesline, moving in the wind.

CHAPTER TWENTY-FIVE

My visit with my sister in Nova Scotia was very cloistered. I did not see much of the province but stayed close to Mattie's house, to Mattie's life. I got into the habit of taking long walks with the baby and sometimes alone. There was a small farm two miles from her home, and I liked to sit up on a fence and watch the horses being broken in or the cows grazing in the pasture. I could see why Mattie liked it here. I understood the beauty this place held for her. The colors were different than back home, more muted. There was a tint of blue in the greenness, a deeper gray to the sky.

At another time in my life, when I was younger, perhaps, I might have seen my sister as romantic, living here alone with her baby. But there was nothing romantic about her life. And now I saw her for what she was, abandoned and sad and, even with her child, as solitary as ever.

It occurred to me that she had fled home thinking she might be able to drop the pain en route to someplace new. Thinking she might be able to scatter it from the back of a motorcycle in bits and pieces, like ashes.

The days I spent with my sister drew us together. There were still times when she seemed remote, but mostly she had come out of herself, and this I knew was because of the baby.

"Tell me about your boyfriend," she said one evening.

"How do you know I have a boyfriend?"

"Well, I'm not sure, but you haven't taken off that khaki shirt for days, and at times you look a little dreamy to me."

"I don't know if he's really my boyfriend," I said. The other night I had lain awake, thinking of Max, and I realized I'd been away from him now longer than I'd known him. At times I couldn't even see his face clearly. But then I'd get a flash of him, like the first bold sketch of a painting. I'd see him sitting next to me on the Ferris wheel or shifting gears in his car or drawing me close to kiss me. And the whole sense of him, of who he was, would come rushing back to me. And I'd feel weak in my knees and warm all over, my heart fluttering and pounding as if he were near.

"His name is Max," I said, and to say his name

aloud gave me an odd, peculiar thrill. I told her about losing my wallet and about Max coming to the rescue. I told her how funny and generous he was, and how blue his eyes were, seawater blue.

"You miss him," she said.

"Yes. Terribly."

She smiled a funny smile. "I envy you," she said.

One morning, a few days before I was to leave, Mattie showed me some sketches she'd done of the baby. There was one in particular I liked, a profile of Kit playing in the grass. I told her it was my favorite.

"It's for you to keep," she said, handing it to me.

"Really? Thanks."

"Let me fix it so it won't get crushed." She slipped the sketch in between two pieces of cardboard and put tape around the edges.

"Remember when Dad used to give us the cardboard from his shirts to draw on?"

"Yes," she said smiling.

"Remember the pile of change on top of his dresser?"

"Uh, huh, and the box of Chicklets in the top drawer."

"And the tin of lozenges he'd bring us when we had sore throats."

"Black currant pastilles," she said. They were made of sugar and black currant juice and they had the consistency of jujube candy.

"They were delicious," I said. "Almost worth the

pain of a sore throat." We were both quiet for a moment thinking of our father.

"It's so sad," I said. "It's so sad that Dad and Mom never got to see Kit. And they'll never see my children or Jay's."

"I know," she said. "It makes me unhappy, too."

"I wish you'd come home with me, Mattie," I said suddenly, surprising us both. "It would be so great for us all to be together."

"I can't come home, Kate," she said. "Let's not talk about it anymore."

On the last day of my visit the three of us drove to Annapolis Royal so Mattie could do some errands, and afterward we had tea in an old inn overlooking Fort Anne. The inn was lovely and sunny, with flowery curtains and antique furniture. The linen was pink damask, and there were little vases with fresh-cut flowers on every table. We had tea and scones and strawberries, and the baby drank warmed milk from her bottle. Later we went for a walk, pushing Kit along in her stroller.

"I feel badly that I haven't shown you anything," Mattie said.

"That's all right, I came to see you." We passed by an old church, and Kit dropped her bottle. When I bent down to pick it up I saw that she was sleeping.

"What are you thinking?" Mattie said.

"That I'm going to miss you and the baby."

"Me, too. Can't you stay a few days longer?"

"No, school starts next week."

"Oh." We walked a little farther, each of us with one hand on the stroller.

"I hate to leave you," I said. I thought of winter coming, and the long, snowy days she'd have to spend alone with the baby. "Come home with me tomorrow," I said.

"Oh, no, I couldn't leave now. I have too much to do."

"Well, at least think about it, Mattie. Okay? Because you could come home," I said. "You could come home if you wanted."

Early in the evening as I was packing I heard my sister call me excitedly. "Kate, Kate, come quick!" I ran outside and saw the baby taking a step toward Mattie. She had a surprised look on her face. She only took two more mini-steps before she fell down, but they were her first steps.

"What a big girl, what a big girl you are!" Mattie kept saying over and over, hugging Kit to her. I stood in the doorway and clapped my hands, and the baby looked from me to Mattie and then she laughed.

"This is cause for celebration," I said. I rummaged through the kitchen and found enough ingredients to bake an apple pie. We had bread and cheese for supper and hot apple pie for dessert. After supper the baby and I sat on Mattie's bed while Mattie went through her closet.

"Here, I want you to take this," she said tossing me a black dress made of crushed velvet. "Do you like it?"

"Yes, thanks."

"Good, and take this sweater, too." It was a cotton pullover with a crew neck. A burgundy color.

"Matt?"

"Yes?"

"What do you think about coming with me?"

"I don't know, Kate."

"Don't you want Kit to see her great-aunt and her uncle? Don't you want her to be around other people?" She sat down on the edge of the bed.

"You make it sound easy."

"Just come home for a visit. You don't have to stay long. It's time, Mattie. It's really time."

"I don't know what to do," she said. And I knew she wanted to go but was afraid.

"You can't expect us to come to you forever," I said. The baby started crawling toward the edge of the bed, and I pulled her back.

"All right," she said, so softly I could hardly hear her.

"You'll come?"

"Yes."

"Really?" She nodded. "You won't change your mind tomorrow?"

"No."

"You're sure?"

"I'm sure."

I lifted the baby up in my arms and waltzed her around the room.

"What are you doing?" Mattie said, laughing.

"I'm teaching her to dance."

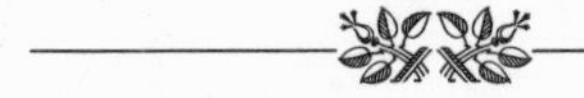

CHAPTER TWENTY-SIX

Mattie and Kit and I arrived in Bar Harbor at ten the next evening. The ferry ride had seemed especially long because the weather was bad and we could not stay out on deck.

Once in Maine, we drove for hours looking for a motel to spend the night, but every place we stopped was booked.

"Let's go a little farther," Mattie said, but there weren't any vacant signs, and we ended up sleeping in the car.

Early the next morning we stopped at a doughnut shop and bought milk and juice for the baby and a bag full of jelly doughnuts. The day was cool and overcast.

"Good driving weather," I said.

"Yes," said Mattie, but she was distracted, and I knew she was nervous about coming home.

I sat in the back with the baby, entertaining her with toys, and when she became fussy I sang to her. Mattie was quiet. By the time we reached Massachusetts we were all exhausted from the long drive.

"Let's stop for a minute," Mattie said. "Okay?"

"Fine." We pulled over at a roadside stand to stretch our legs and give the baby room to move around. A young girl was selling lemonade and bouquets of fresh-cut flowers, marigolds and sweet Williams the color of raspberries. Mattie bought two bouquets. When we were less than an hour from home we stopped at a gas station so we could wash up. The baby had pear smeared all over her shirt and in her hair. There were fast-food cartons, Styrofoam cups, and zweiback biscuits strewn all over the backseat of the car. Mattie took the baby into the washroom, and I cleaned up the car.

When Mattie came out I saw she had changed her shirt and brushed her hair. The baby, too, was in a new outfit, and her face was so clean it was shiny.

"I had to wash her hair to get the food out," Mattie said.

"I did my best with the car. But you really need a vacuum."

"I know," she said. She took a deep breath. "Well, I guess we'd better go."

"Yes," I said. "There's no point in hanging around here." I was anxious to get home. I was dying to see Georgia and Jay and Celia, too. I was also hoping that there might be a letter from Max.

"It's so strange to be back," Mattie said. The closer we got to home, the more pensive she became. "I couldn't do this without you."

"It'll be okay."

When we drove through the town of West Stockbridge, Mattie said, "Look at all these new stores!"

"I know. Georgia's is here now."

"Since when?"

"Oh, for a few years."

She was driving at a snail's pace, and I wanted to yell at her to hurry up. When we hit the hill to our house, I had to stop myself from leaping out of the car and running all the way. Georgia's Jeep was there but not Jay's car. Then I remembered: It was Monday and he'd be at the pharmacy.

As soon as the car stopped I jumped out. "Georgia, Georgia!" I yelled, rushing back to the garden. Georgia was bending over her flowers with her garden shears in one hand, her old straw hat on her head.

"Georgia, I'm home," I said.

She spun around at the sound of my voice. "Oh, Kate," she said, dropping everything. We ran to one another and embraced. She held me close against her. "How did you get here? I thought you were coming tomorrow."

"Well . . . I have a surprise for you," I said, but she didn't hear me. I saw her hands tremble, and then I knew that she'd seen Mattie. She was standing at the end of the garden with the baby on her hip, her arms full of flowers.

"Mattie," Georgia said, and then she was weeping uncontrollably and Mattie was hurrying to her. Very gently Mattie put her arm around Georgia's neck and kissed her cheek.

"Hello, Georgia," she said. Her eyes filled with tears. They stood there, looking at each other for a long moment, and then Georgia wiped her eyes and said, "And who is this sweet bundle?"

"Katharine. I call her Kit."

"Hello, Kit," Georgia said. The baby reached out her hand to touch Georgia's hat. Three generations, I thought. Three generations of women.

I was about to go inside when I heard the sound of a car coming up the hill. I ran around to the front of the house.

"Jay! Jay!"

"Hello, Kate." He was happy to see me. I gave him a big hug. "When did you get back?"

"Just now."

"Who's car?" he asked, eyeing the Mustang.

"Mattie's."

"She's here?"

"Yes." I took his arm and pulled him around to the back of the house. Mattie turned to us.

"Hello, Jay," she said. "My God, you're so tall."

He smiled, and I saw that they were afraid of each other. "Hello, Mattie."

She took a step toward him, shyly.

"It's good to see you, Jay," she whispered.

"You, too," he said. They were both trying not to cry. "Who are *you*?" he said to Kit. "You're awfully pretty." The baby stared at him without blinking.

"This is Kit," Mattie said.

As if on cue, the baby started crying, and Mattie said she was tired from the long trip.

"Did I get any mail, Georgia?" I asked.

"What?"

"Did I get any mail?" I turned to Jay.

"I don't know. Maybe she'd like to play with my keys?" he said to Mattie. He reached into his pocket.

I left them standing in the garden, and I ran inside the house. On the kitchen table was a pile of mail. I leafed through it all till I came to a letter addressed to me in an oddly slanted script. I ripped it open and read.

Dear Kate,

I miss you. Being on the road just isn't the same without you. Everytime I see something interesting I wish you were with me, so that we could see it together. How was your boat ride and your trip to Nova Scotia? How's your sister?

By the time you get this letter I'll be in New Orleans. As soon as I know where I'll be staying I'll write you.

I have to be back East at the end of October.

Maybe I could stop by on my way home to see you. We could go trick-or-treating together, ha ha.

Kate, if you want to know the truth, I've been going crazy thinking of you all the time and missing you. Please write back and let me know how you feel about me, or if I'm just alone in this. I hope not.

Take good care of yourself, Grace. And don't let anyone else steal your wallet.

All my love,
Max

I let out a whoop.

"What is it? What is it now?" Georgia said coming inside. She held the baby securely under one arm. Mattie and Jay followed behind.

"Nothing," I said throwing my arms around her. "I'm just so happy to be home."

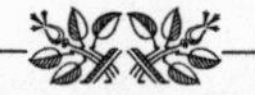

Elissa Haden Guest

has worked as a nursery school teacher and has written for the Children's Television Workshop. Her first novel, *The Handsome Man*, was highly praised by reviewers and by Robert Cromier, who said "young Alexandra Barnes is an irresistible heroine. The prose crackles and pops—but suddenly you find yourself with a lump in your throat. What a funny, tender, and, in the end, moving novel."

Ms. Guest and her husband, a film editor, live in New York and Los Angeles with their young daughter.

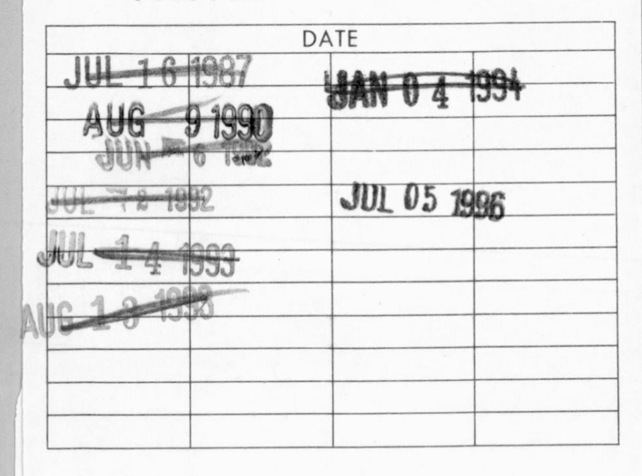